IN QUAKING HILLS

THE TRAVELS OF SCOUT SHANNON

KATE MACLEOD

Cover image by Benjamin P. Roque.

Ratatoskr Press logo by Aidan Vincent Kise

ISBN 978-1-946552-53-2

❀ Created with Vellum

1

AFTER SPENDING the last four days of her life hiding out from a deadly solar particle storm in an underground bunker, trapped inside with six treacherous women and a trio of girl assassins, it would be terribly ironic if Scout Shannon died now, plunging headlong into a ditch, because she had never learned to drive.

But Scout wasn't in a place to appreciate that irony. Not with the front end of the massive rover tipping dizzyingly down into the ravine despite her pushing, pulling, and stomping on every control she could find. She had nothing in her stomach except an excess of coffee, but even that was threatening to come back again, the bitterness washing up against her back teeth in spite of her best attempts to swallow it back down. Her hands were so slick with sweat they slipped over the control yoke. She hooked her forearms through it and pulled back as hard as she could, mentally begging for the rover to reverse away from the cliff already.

She wasn't even sure that was the right thing to do.

The rover hung for a moment, teetering back and forth on the edge of the ravine. She could see loose rocks bounding down past her on either side, first a few bouncing and skittering randomly, but then more like a wave. Entire sheets of gravel were sliding off the hillside to plunge down into the ravine. It was a surreal sight, like the hill was melting, rock like hot wax pouring over jutting boulders and past scrubby trees whose tenacious roots clung stubbornly to the rock face.

Years of sheering winds had twisted the trunks of those little trees into knobby, spiraling shapes that branched off at random. Now those branches shook like the bony arms of ghosts attempting to scare this new disaster away but never succumb to it. Scout wasn't sure whether she found those defiant trees frightening or comforting. It would, she decided, largely depend on whether she, like the trees, stayed firm or if she was washed away in the tidal wave of loose topsoil.

The two dogs in the rover's cockpit with Scout were barking like mad. The movement of the rover wasn't what was bothering them— they had started barking a moment before Scout had lurched over the unseen obstruction in the trail and lost control of the vehicle— although the rocking *was* tossing them about ruthlessly. Scout was belted into the driver's seat, but the two dogs were trying desperately to hold themselves still even as they kept barking, heads tipped back as if they were addressing their warning to the sky at large.

Gert, a dark-haired mix of unknown dog breeds, was more or less wedged between the passenger seat and the front console of the rover. Her large head repeatedly impacted against the hard edge of the console, but she didn't wince or even seem to notice. The rat terrier, named Shadow despite his mainly white coloring, was smaller and nearly went tumbling back into the main body of the rover. Scout had to take a hand off the yoke to catch him by the collar before he went flying down the steps. He yelped briefly in surprise, but then resumed his anxious barking.

What had set them off in the first place? Scout didn't have a clue. She tucked the little dog close against her stomach and got her hand back on the yoke. Not that there was anything she could do now with none of the rover's treads actually on the ground.

Besides make things worse. She could usually find a way to manage that.

The rover was still rocking back and forth, the long drop to the bottom of the ravine dipping in and out of view in front of her. The landslide of rocks around her was unceasing. If the rover tipped either way, if its treads touched down on that moving surface, would she be carried away like driftwood on the tide?

No, surely the rover, built to comfortably house a group of four researchers on a long-term expedition, was too heavy to be dislodged so easily.

Still, there was more going on here than her lousy driving. They had hit something, or something had hit them. Had the dogs been barking even before then? Scout wasn't sure. Her memory of the two events overlapped and refused to settle into a definable sequence.

The teetering slowed, then the rover balanced for a moment at an untenable forty-five-degree angle before settling back on its rear treads. Scout made extra certain she had the engine in reverse before slowly easing her foot down on the pedal. The rover rolled back away from the edge. When the windscreen no longer showed even a hint of the plummet to her death that had been in store for her a moment before, she braked the rover and killed the engine.

Scout slumped over the yoke, trembling all over. She wasn't nearly recovered enough after the events of the last four days for such stresses. She pressed the heels of her palms to her eyes, but despite the terror still making her heart pound, no tears came. She was too exhausted for more emotions, apparently.

Once her heart had slowed, she pulled her hands from her face and looked to her dogs. Gert had stopped her frighteningly deep barks, those low rumbles that made her seem particularly hellhoundish. Shadow was still barking now and again, but with the air of a guardian unsure if the danger was really past. Scout put a comforting hand on his head and he gave one last halfhearted woof before settling down onto her lap.

Poor fellow. As bad as those days underground had been for her, they had come far too close to killing Shadow. Scout picked him up in her arms and carried him down to the back of the rover where the stacks of bunks were. She laid him at the foot of the bottom bunk and he curled up on the faded quilt there, turning round and round before finally settling down and tucking his nose under his own paw.

Gert, standing at Scout's heels, made an inquiring sound. From the head of the bed the cat Tubbins made an equally inquisitive mew and

Gert, her worry over Shadow now completely forgotten, tried to leap past Scout to get at the cat she had nearly killed days before. Scout stopped her with a well-placed knee.

"Come on, Gert," she said, catching the dog's collar until she had her attention. Gert was twice Shadow's size, but really still a puppy. When she was growling that fearsome growl it was easy to forget how young and innocent she was, but when she looked up at Scout like she was doing now with those warm brown eyes, it was hard to remember she was ever anything but cute and harmless.

Scout pressed the button that caused the door to emerge from its recess, creating a little square of space between the dining nook and the bunks. It rolled out about half a meter, then the door swung open, letting in the full blaze of the midmorning sun.

Scout started sweating at once, and she wasn't even outside yet. But, hot as the air was, she stopped first to pull on the new long-sleeved sun-protective shirt she had found when scrounging for usable items back in Viola's compound before she had blown the explosives that had blocked all the ways out, the closest she could get to giving those she had left behind a proper burial. The shirt fell midway down her thighs, barely past her cargo shorts, but she smeared sunscreen on her bare calves. She settled her father's battered old bush hat on her head before leaping down to the ground. Gert jumped down after her, less than graceful, but unbothered by her hard landing.

Scout looked up the slope of the hill behind the rover. What had been old, fractured rock covered with loose grit and sparse crabgrass was now just bare, somewhat more fractured rock. Like someone had swept the ground smooth. Everything remotely loose was all at the bottom of the ravine now.

There was no way she had done all that damage with the rover. And after backtracking a ways along the trail she had been following and finding no obstruction, Scout was beginning to doubt she had hit anything either.

Something had made her lurch, lurch hard and nearly tumble over the cliff. And it had shaken everything around them loose, hard enough to make it all fall away in a sheet. What could do such a thing?

Scout had heard of earthquakes. The southeastern cities on the ocean sometimes reported them. She had never experienced one herself; no one had, not this far north and west. The land was flat here, nothing but prairie all the way to the horizon, split down the middle by the narrow spine of hills she had just been crossing.

Had she just experienced an earthquake?

Then a second thought hit her, sending a chill rippling over her skin despite the already stifling heat of the day. Was it going to happen again?

Scout whistled for Gert and then climbed back into the rover. Just in case, she'd rather be back out on the flat prairie on the far side of the hills as soon as possible. If that was an earthquake, there might be others, and she'd rather be out in the flat grasslands when it struck.

Besides, she had a destination to reach. More than that, she had a mission. And her clock was ticking.

Liam McGillicuddy, the galactic marshal she had been trading messages with, was coming to meet her in three days. His partner, Gertrude Bauer, had died during the solar storm, but she had saved Scout's life before losing her own. Scout was taking care of all of Gertrude's things, her gun and badge, but also other assorted equipment, all attached to a belt Scout wore around her own hips now. She was sure Liam was coming to get it all back; it seemed too valuable not to recover. Some other galactic marshal would probably be carrying all of it soon.

But perhaps Liam himself was coming not just to get the belt, but also to meet the girl his partner had died for. And Scout would introduce him to the dog she had named in Gertrude's honor.

Scout didn't know why he was coming in person, or what he intended to do, or what she should expect. She had written him a long message telling him everything that had happened since she had met his partner out on a hillside the moment before the solar storm had started. She had reported every poisoning, stabbing, and accidental death that had gone down over the last four days.

His response had been terse: just a set of coordinates and the words MEET ME.

Scout didn't know what that meant or why he couldn't say more.

But his prior exchanges with Gertrude said he was not a terse man. There had to be a reason.

Scout had spent the days after Gertrude's death, the days she was still trapped underground by the ongoing coronal mass ejection event bathing the surface of her planet with deadly solar particles, researching Gertrude's last mission, the one she had left uncompleted. It had not been an official mission. Technically, she had been on a long-overdue vacation. In reality, she had been chasing down a man that she had caught once before but who had later gone free on a technicality.

Gertrude had known he was guilty; her own grandmother was among those he had conned and left destitute on a forgotten world even harsher than Scout's home world of Amatheon. So Gertrude had taken a leave of absence to chase him. Scout got the sense that her boss had pretended not to know what she was really up to. She doubted he would be able to do the same for Liam if he tried to finish what Gertrude had started. Two galactic marshals using their vacation time to pursue the same personal vendetta was probably the sort of thing that would get a boss in trouble from the bigger boss, Scout guessed. Maybe that was why his reply had been so short. His boss might be reading his messages to be sure he didn't break any rules.

But Scout could. She could find the con man in the next three days and drag him to where Liam was going to land his ship to meet her. Gertrude had accumulated more evidence; it was all on the tablet in a pouch on the belt. That evidence plus the recaptured culprit—Scout didn't know anything about galactic law, but surely that would be enough.

She knew all the steps to take to find this man and bring him to Liam. She was less sure what to do with the two data disks hidden deep in her front pocket. She couldn't read them herself, but she knew they contained information that the Planet Dwellers wanted, the Space Farers had proved they would kill for, and the rebellion that lurked in the hills had attempted to secure for their own uses.

Scout didn't know which of the three she could trust. She was pretty sure it was none of the above. For now, she kept the secrets others had died for safe in her pocket, where she could always feel them pressing into her thigh. Maybe she could ask Liam what she should do.

If he turned out to be trustworthy. Scout couldn't be sure until she met him.

Scout looked down at the navigation screen, then got the rover rolling again in the direction of the flashing dot. Prairie Springs. Nothing more than an unremarkable little town in the middle of the grasslands. She had visited on a few occasions before, she seemed to remember, but she was only heading that way because it was the closest town to the hidden compound where she had waited out the storm.

But she also knew Ruby, the woman who ran the public house in this town, and Ruby had access to the network run by all the public houses in all the towns. If anyone had seen her quarry, that network would know and could point her in the right direction.

Scout sat back in her seat, starting to relax now that the trail was flattening out and the grass around her was changing from the stunted, scrubby tufts of the hill country to the tall, waving stalks of the prairie. She wanted justice for Gertrude, but that wasn't the only reason she was going to find this guy. She also kind of hoped that if she showed up to the rendezvous with the fugitive in tow, Liam might be impressed with her skill and gumption, and he might be just a little more inclined to finish that other thing Gertrude had left undone.

Gertrude had promised to take Scout off this world, to show her the galaxy. And now the thought that had never entered her mind before four days ago was her entire focus. She *had* to leave this place. And finding this man, this Farlane McFarlane, was her key.

2

THE SUN WAS APPROACHING its zenith when Prairie Springs finally came into view. Scout could just make out the roof of the public house —the tallest building in most towns—over the nodding heads of the tall grasses making a golden tunnel over the narrow trail. On her bike she'd be almost completely enclosed by the grasses, but in the rover she was higher, the tops of the grain still below even the level of her feet. Scout wasn't used to this perspective, but she judged she had a few minutes yet before she reached her destination.

Her stomach growled, frustrated at the all-coffee diet she had been subsisting on since before dawn. But Shadow had come up the steps some time ago to curl up on her lap and she didn't want to wake him. She looked around the driver's seat. The rover's prior owners, the Planet Dweller Ottilie and her Space Farer companion Ebba, had lived in this vehicle full time, always on the move. Surely they had stashed some food up here in the cockpit?

Scout found a little compartment under the console just to the left of her left knee and tapped it open. Sure enough: protein bars. Scout took one and tore off the label without glancing at it. The different flavors were beyond her palate's ability to discern, anyway. She took a large bite of the bar and tried not to involve her tongue much as she chewed it. The food was technically nonperishable, but in her lifelong experience, every bar tasted like dust, anyway.

Amatheon was in a perpetual state of being one good harvest away from real bounty. Even Scout, young and mostly uneducated as she was, knew that it was odd for an agricultural planet to import most of its food from other parts of the galaxy. Years of listening to grown-ups debate politics had yet to give her any answers as to why this was still the situation after more than a century of colonization. She doubted she would ever understand it.

But it didn't really matter. Whatever it took, when Liam landed at the meeting point in three days, she was going to convince him to take her away from here. This had stopped being her home the day her parents and baby brother died. All the years in between had been just her waiting to go.

And she was so ready to go. She didn't really belong to any particular place anymore. She had been born under the dome of a city, but that city was gone now. Obliterated. Nothing remained save a crater the prairie grass had not yet reclaimed. She had been just a kid when it still stood, but she still remembered the gleaming whiteness of the city, the prefabricated buildings dropped from space and assembled on the surface. Like a child's building blocks, they had only come in a few basic shapes, but could be combined in infinite varieties. Cities had wide boulevards with fountains and overflowing planters, long straight roads lined with businesses grouped into districts, and endless twisting alleyways full of surprises, both wonderful and otherwise.

But towns on Amatheon weren't simply small versions of cities. They had never been part of the prefabricated colonization plans. They had sprung up wherever people had gotten sick of life under the domes. Everything about the towns was different from the cities, starting with the fact that they were open to the world around them. Cities were accessible only through a small number of highly controlled gates. Towns, on the other hand, usually had a wall like Prairie Springs had to separate farmland from town and to keep the wind from filling the town with clouds of dust and wheat chaff. But in Prairie Springs, rather than a gate, there was a gateway, nothing more than an opening in the wall with no door and no guard.

The gate into Prairie Springs was too narrow for the rover, so Scout pulled off the road to park out of the way against the wall. Gert sleeping at her feet made it difficult to work the pedals, but she managed a respectably neat stop before killing the engine. The sudden loss of the engine's hum was almost deafening and woke both the dogs.

Shadow yawned with a squeak, then hopped off Scout's lap to stretch himself out. He had gotten a bit thinner over the last few days, but the muscles under his white fur were as tight as ever. He looked up at her, his dark eyes peering out of the bandit mask pattern of the black spot covering his head. Then he ran down the stairs to the back of the rover. Gert followed, the white tip at the very end of her tail a blur, the entire back half of her sleek black body wiggling back and forth as it powered that thumping wag.

"You guys are going to stay here," she said to the dogs, who had both started jumping excitedly the moment she put on the old bush hat. Shadow sat down, his posture straight and formal. He knew what she meant. Gert just kept wagging her tail. It thumped so loudly against the leg of the kitchen table it must be hurting her, but she didn't seem to mind. She looked up at Scout as if she really wished she knew what Scout meant.

Scout sighed. She needed to make training this dog a priority. "Sit, Gert," she said. Shadow stiffened his already perfect sitting form, but Gert missed the hint. "Never mind," Scout said. "I'll just be a minute."

She went over to the bunk beds built into the back of the rover and leaned into the bottom one. "Hello, Tubbins," Scout said. The cat gave a soft mew. Scout gathered him up, pillow and all, and put him gently inside an empty plastic crate. She tapped the opening mechanism on the door with her elbow, keeping Gert back with her knee as the dog tried to get a better look at the cat in the crate in her arms. The cat hissed his displeasure. The two were most decidedly not friends.

"Down, Gert," Scout said. As soon as the door was open wide enough, she stepped out, dropping to the ground nearly a meter below. She turned back to the rover. "Stay, dogs," she commanded, then jabbed the mechanism to shut the door. Shadow remained as he was at formal attention, but Gert stood at the edge of the rover with her head out the door until the closing metal hatch finally forced her to step back.

Her eyes on Scout's were full of abandoned hurt. Then the hatch clicked shut.

Crate in arms, Scout walked through the gate into the town proper. Prairie Springs had grown since she had been here last. New homes built from prefabricated panels crowding into the spaces between the older homes built from repurposed storage containers. The Space Farer logo that had once adorned the containers had mostly been scrubbed away, but a few faded stylized rockets remained.

If things kept going like they had been, there would be a renewed zest among the Planet Farers for removing those soon. Scout hoped to be gone long before that point. She had seen enough Planet Dweller–versus–Space Farer conflict in the last four days to last her a lifetime.

When she reached the public house in the center of town, she saw that the massive doors angled into the ground on both sides of the base of the building had been thrown open wide to let air pass through. Scout could imagine that after four days of all the townspeople huddling together down there to wait out the solar storm, it needed a good airing out.

A group of children streamed in and out of the open doors that led underground, carrying out old laundry and empty containers and bringing in canisters filled with water and food from the back of the public house. It used to be that the coronal mass ejection events only reached the surface during rare, powerful storms, every year or so. Now they were happening more and more often. They lasted longer and were more powerful, too intense to risk being caught out of doors as Scout so nearly had.

This planet was scarcely habitable anymore, particularly not for a nomad like Scout. She couldn't wait to leave it behind.

Scout climbed the steps to the public house, pausing in the doorway to let her eyes adjust to the dark interior. A public house was always dark compared to the bright sun outside; having once been a separate compartment of the spaceship that had brought the first settlers to Amatheon, it had no windows. After the cities had been established, the empty compartments were dropped from orbit, scattered in a network around the cities to house the early explorers when they ventured out from under the domes. The satellites that created the protective shield against radiation hadn't been completed in those days, and it was crucial that the explorers always had a shelter close at hand in case of solar storms.

After the days of the explorers, the compartments had briefly been supply depots, little used and in danger of being forgotten entirely. But just in the last few decades, there had been a movement—nothing organized, just a general dissatisfaction with city life that led to more and more people living outside of the domes. The public houses, with their ability to protect from coronal mass ejection events, were the obvious choice for shelter.

Now the towns had largely outgrown that confined space, spreading out into separate buildings, but the structure that no longer actually housed the public was still the center of town life. Now they were part meeting place, part general store, and part bar. Scout's work delivering packages on her bike had largely been between such public houses. The proprietors maintained a communication network so shortages in one community could be alleviated by supplies from another.

But they also used them for gossip.

"Can I help you?" a woman asked.

Scout's sun-dazzled eyes took a moment to pick out the speaker, a woman with massive arms and red hair pulled into something between a ponytail and a bun. She was the proprietor, Ruby Collins. She had also once been one of Scout's mother's closest friends, back before she died.

"Hey," Scout said, stepping up to set the crate on the counter.

Ruby peered at her suspiciously for a moment before her eyes lit up with recognition. "As I live and breathe, Scout Shannon!" she exclaimed. "I almost didn't recognize you. I thought someone had stolen your father's hat!"

"It's been a few years," Scout admitted.

"More than that," Ruby said, coming around the counter to gather Scout up in a stifling hug. "You're shooting up like a weed." She released Scout from the hug but grasped both of Scout's arms to hold her still as she looked right into Scout's eyes. "You're older in lots of ways, I reckon. You weather this last storm okay?"

"Well enough," Scout said. "I sheltered with some strangers with political issues they took out on each other."

"Sounds miserable," Ruby said, then tapped the crate. "What's this?"

"Just a cat that fell into my care. I can't keep him, of course. The dogs are more than enough work. I have two now. I was hoping you might know someone who'd take him? He's old, but healthy. Goes by the name Tubbins."

"Hello, Tubbins," Ruby said, reaching into the crate to pull out the large orange cat. Tubbins was purring loudly. She turned him around in her hands to look into his yellow eyes. "I reckon I can take him. Could stand the company. It gets too quiet here at night now that the kids have grown."

"Thanks," Scout said. That was one responsibility she could check off her list.

"How much you want for him?" Ruby asked.

"He's not mine to sell," Scout said. "But I was hoping you could help me with another thing."

"Surely," Ruby said, cradling the cat in her arms and scratching all around his ears. Tubbins purred in perfect bliss.

Scout took the tablet off her belt and set it on the counter, then pulled a single round reflective lens out of her pocket and placed it over her left eye. She closed her right eye as she tapped her way through the tablet's menus. Ruby was frowning slightly as she watched. From what she could see, Scout was tapping away at a blank gray slab.

Scout found the photograph she was searching for and turned the tablet to face Ruby. She plucked the lens from where it had adhered to her face and held it out for Ruby.

"You have to look with this," she explained.

Ruby looked skeptical, but she took the lens and copied Scout's gestures. "Where did you get this?" Ruby asked, fascinated. Scout knew the feeling. This technology was far beyond anything they had on their remote, rural planet.

"It was sort of a gift from one of the strangers I waited out the storm with," Scout said. "Have you seen the man in the photo?"

Ruby was looking around the room, watching as the display inside the lens fed her impossible amounts of information about the world around her: how far away everything was, the temperature and humidity of the air, the time of day to the nanosecond. Scout nudged the tablet a little closer and Ruby finally looked down at it. It looked like a featureless stone tablet to Scout now, but she knew that Ruby, with the lens on her face, could see the image of a man staring up at her.

"Can't say that I have," Ruby said after a moment's consideration, plucking the lens from her face and dropping it next to the tablet. "Far-lane McFarlane. Sounds like a fake name. He's distinctive-looking, though, isn't he? With that twist to the end of his nose. Let me ask the network," Ruby said, disappearing into her office behind the counter, the cat still nestled contentedly in her arms.

Scout put the tablet and the lens away, looking back over her shoulder as something momentarily blocked out the sun streaming through the doorway. Someone must have just walked past; there was no one behind her now. Scout pushed back her battered bush hat to run a hand through her short blonde curls that had been molded down with sweat. She had only been out of the controlled environment of the rover's interior for a few moments, and already she was a stinky mess.

"I've got a lead for you," Ruby said, emerging from the back room and pouring the cat back into the pillow-lined crate. "You know Flat Valley, just north of here?"

"I think so," Scout said, although she wasn't sure. It didn't matter; she wasn't alone on her bike anymore. The rover's navigation system would tell her the way.

"Yolanda in Flat Valley knows your fellow. He's not what you call a regular, but she's seen him more than once. No one there knows who he is or what he's doing for a living. He comes into town for supplies now and again. Just food, nothing suspicious, but they don't like strangers in those parts. It's a bit north of here." She gave Scout a significant look and Scout nodded. She knew what Ruby was saying. North meant further from the cities. The people out that way tended toward a certain stubborn independence. They had fled from the people who had fled the cities in the first place.

"Thanks," Scout said. She started toward the door, but turned back. "Say, Ruby, did you guys feel an earthquake about midmorning?"

"An earthquake? Here?" Ruby asked.

Scout nodded.

"We don't get earthquakes in these parts."

"That's what I thought. Still, something weird happened on the road here. Any strange rumors from the hills?"

"Just the usual," Ruby said. "Bandits robbing folks. Rebels doing whatever it is that rebels do. If that's the way you are going, you take care."

"I will," Scout said. "It was good seeing you." She didn't add, "one last time."

Scout settled her hat back on her head before stepping outside, hands in her pockets as she walked back to the town gate.

Beyond the town walls, the villagers were running farm machinery, harvesting the overripe grain. The constant whir of the motors filled the air, punctuated by bursts of thrashing sounds as the grain was pulled through.

Then Scout heard something else, something not quite drowned out by the roar of the machines.

Something was wrong. Her dogs were barking. Not happy barks or even warning barks. These were barks of raw panic.

She pulled her hands from her pockets and broke into a run.

3

THE ROVER WAS TALLER than the wall, and even from inside the town, Scout could see it was parked just where she had left it, off to one side of the road near the gateway. Still, there was something about its dark silhouette against the bright blue of the midday sky, like a bad omen. Something in the way it hovered over that part of the town, not letting the sun reach the wall to reflect blindingly back from the sheets of metal. Like it was creating its own little patch of darkness.

But some of that darkness was her own vision. Just a few days ago, she had nearly died when someone pulled all the air out of the room she had been hiding in. She had recovered, but she still had headaches and nightmares. She wasn't well enough to be running again and her brain seemed prepared to knock her unconscious if that's what it took to make her stop.

Scout clenched her hands into fists and kept her feet moving despite the frightening way her heart was pounding in her chest. Normally she loved that feeling, when she had pedaled as fast as she could for as long as she could, but this time it was different. It was like there was another muscle, some foreign muscle, wrapped around her heart, squeezing and squeezing. Choking. She could feel a wet warmth in her chest, like her heart was beginning to ooze out her own blood because of the squeezing.

But she wouldn't faint. She wouldn't stop. Her dogs needed her.

She burst out of the gateway, sending up a small cloud of reddish dust as she changed direction, then an even larger one as she skidded to a halt.

The door to the rover was standing wide open. Not how she had left it. A boy was standing in the open doorway, tossing a bag down to another boy on the ground. It jangled when he caught it. He handed it over to a girl no more than ten, who stacked it with a few others on the back of a wagon.

Scout had encountered their kind before, but only in the domed cities. Still, they looked the same as those she had known in the cities. They all had bedraggled hair, clothes either too large or too small but always old and faded to near unusability, and only half of them had anything at all on their feet. And yet, could you call them street kids, here where there were no streets?

Scout didn't know quite what to do. They appeared to be robbing her, but then none of it was really her stuff. She had taken the crates of food, clothing, and medicine from the compound, since Viola, being dead, didn't need them anymore. The crates full of broken machines and electronics had belonged to Ottilie and Ebba, who were also quite dead and needed none of them anymore. Thievery was a bit rude, but while Scout had never considered herself a street kid, they were all orphans like her. In a way, they were like her younger siblings. Annoying, and yet she felt compelled to take care of them as much as she could.

She had taken it all with her because she hadn't wanted it to go to waste when she buried the compound. Why not just let them have it?

Then Shadow yelped in pain. It took a moment for her eyes to find him. He was no longer in the rover but was crouched under one of the front treads. A girl in a small, belly-bearing T-shirt and shorts that didn't quite want to stay around her narrow hips was poking at him with a stick. Scout saw a bleeding bite wound on her shin but could summon little sympathy. No doubt that girl had earned it.

"Leave my dog alone," Scout said.

The girl ignored her, trying to poke Shadow again. Not poke—
spear. She was out for blood.

Even ill as she was, the speed of her reflexes was undiminished. Scout had her slingshot in her hand and fired a stone at the girl within one blink of an eye. The stone struck the ground just in front of the girl's bare foot, sending up a plume of dust.

"Leave my dog alone," Scout said again, a little louder than before. She started to take a step forward when she heard the distinctive whistle of a stone flying far too close to her ear, close enough to make the brim of her hat tremble.

"There are more of us than there are of you," the boy on the ground said. He had no slingshot, but at the range they were from each other, he didn't much need one. He had another stone in his hand, ready to throw if she moved.

"I can't argue with your math," Scout said, holding her hands where he could see them, empty slingshot in one hand, no stone in the other. With that stone in his hand ready to hurl at her, she couldn't risk more than a few quick, furtive glances at the rest of the scene around him, but she could see no sign of Gert. "Hey, Mr. Math. I had another dog?"

"That dog bit me," the spear girl said, sounding near tears.

"I bet she did," Scout said. Gert had bitten her, not Shadow. Trying to stab him with a spear was so loathsome an act that Scout felt sick to her stomach just thinking of it. If she would stab an innocent dog, what would she do to one that had bitten her? "Where is she?"

The kids looked at each other without speaking. Their air of sullen guilt was making Scout's heart race again.

"Where is she?" she repeated.

The little girl near the wagon pointed to one of the sacks, this one on the ground. Scout's rising panic abated only a little when the sack twitched.

"You kids are monsters," Scout said.

"She *bit* me," the girl said again.

"Of *course* she did," Scout said. She could hear the anger creeping into her own voice. "That's hardly an odd thing for her to do when I left her to protect this rover and you decided to rob it."

"The dog's not hurt," the boy she had dubbed Mr. Math said. "She bit Sal, but I tied her up in that sack without hurting her. We just needed her out of the way." Then, almost too softly to be heard: "Sorry."

"*Sorry*?" Scout repeated with a humorless laugh. "Hey, do you kids know what's funny?"

They stared sullenly back at her.

"What's funny is that if you had just asked me for what you needed, I would have given it to you. You didn't need to rob me. You certainly didn't need to attack my dogs."

"How were we supposed to know that?" the boy standing in the rover demanded. He seemed to be the oldest in the bunch. There was even a dark smudge on his upper lip that might be the first hint of a mustache.

"You could have asked," Scout said. "I would have given you everything I could spare. Heck, we could have worked out a deal where I'd've let you keep my rover after I leave here in a few days. Lost opportunity. I hope you've learned something from all this. Now get out of my ride." That last bit dripped with every gram of don't-mess-with-me attitude she could infuse it with.

"What are you going to do? Yell for the grown-ups?" the kid in the rover sneered.

"We still outnumber you," Mr. Math said.

"And we have your dogs," spear girl added. Her voice cracked a bit, like she was trying hard to sound unflappable but wasn't quite there. Then she poked at Shadow again.

Scout dropped the stone she had been hiding in her sleeve for most of their conversation into her hand, then fired with one swift motion, this time catching the girl in her unbitten shin. She dropped the spear and fell to the ground with a cry.

Then Scout staggered back, the wind suddenly knocked out of her. It took a moment to realize that Mr. Math had thrown his stone, catching her right in the chest. She gasped for breath, the corners of her vision threatening to go black again. But through that deepening blackness, she saw the boy pull his arm back to throw another stone. She doubted he had thrown as hard as he could the first time, as much as she knew she was about to have an impressive black and blue patch across her chest that would linger for weeks.

Scout reached to the back of her belt, the belt that had once belonged to a galactic marshal, and drew the laser pistol. She had intended to fire a warning shot, but with her vision still filled with black blossoms and her breath coming in hard gasps, she didn't trust herself not to kill one of them by mistake or maybe even hit one of the dogs.

Luckily for her, just seeing the weapon was warning enough. Scout heard the soft thump of a stone dropping to the dusty ground, the louder thump of the boy jumping out of the rover, and then the scrabble of the two boys helping the spear girl limp away to disappear in the grass, the littler girl who had stood silently beside the wagon all this time scampering after them. The wagon remained silent, abandoned.

Scout put the gun back, feeling more than a little sick. She had just drawn a weapon on kids. *Kids.*

Granted, they had hurt her and tried to hurt her dogs, but was this who she was now? Someone who reacted that quickly with that much disproportionate force?

Still laboring to breathe, Scout staggered forward to fumble at the ties holding Gert's bag closed. At last the dog broke free, knocking Scout to the ground as she jumped up on her, causing another paroxysm of pain to seize Scout's chest. Shadow came slowly out from behind the rover tread, eyes on the tall grass in case his tormentor returned.

"Good dogs," Scout said, trying to scratch them both around the ears at once. As usual, each dog thought it was getting shortchanged in the attention department and fell away from Scout's reach in a loud, growling tussle. "Come on, dogs. Let's get out of here."

Street kids. Another wave of nausea at the thought of what she had almost done.

Scout had been an orphan herself since the age of ten. She had been left with nothing but a bike, a dog, and the clothes on her back, but that had been enough for her. Delivering packages and messages from town to town had kept her and Shadow fed. She had always known a lot of kids who were a lot worse off. In the cities they banded together into groups, groups of such size the city officials took sometimes extreme measures to break them up, to catch strays and lock them away.

For their own good, of course.

She doubted any street kids living in a town could band together like the city kids could. The four she had seen were probably all a town like Prairie Springs could support, however involuntary that support was.

Those kids likely needed whatever they had determined to be valuable more than she would ever need it. She should leave it for them, all of it. Perhaps a little kindness from a stranger would make them rethink how they went about things. Perhaps they would learn to be kinder to dogs, at least.

It wasn't like she could get all that stuff back inside the rover, anyway. Not when it hurt just to move her arms.

But as she got the dogs inside and closed the door between her and Prairie Springs, she knew it was mostly because she felt guilty. She had pulled a gun on a bunch of kids. Without a thought, like it was the most natural thing in the world.

Which, after the last four days she had barely survived, it really was.

Scout made her slow, painful way up to the driving cockpit and set the navigation system to take her to Flat Valley. Then she flopped down on the seat to watch the land around Prairie Springs fall away behind her.

Sitting still was better than moving. It only hurt if she took a deep breath.

She couldn't wait to get off this planet.

Not that she had more than the vaguest idea what life was like anywhere else. Gertrude hadn't talked about it much, but her revulsion to life on Scout's world had spoken volumes. That, and the belt of wondrous gadgets she had left behind, said that the rest of the galaxy had to be infinitely better. Wonderful, even.

Not to mention the clothes Gertrude had worn. She had dressed for rough conditions, intending to walk through the open countryside as she stalked her prey, but even so, her clothes had been finer than anything Scout had ever seen. Touching the long white shirt that had protected her from sun exposure had been like touching a cloud, a brightly glowing white cloud. And when the shirt had gotten dirty—more than dirty, bloody—Gertrude had just run it under water and snapped it in the air, and just like that, it was clean and dry.

Scout might have taken that shirt when she took the belt, but it had been badly torn when Gertrude had died. Being stabbed in the back would do that.

Once Prairie Springs was nothing more than a bad memory behind her, Scout turned her attention back to the navigation system. It was going to take a few hours to get to Flat Valley. It would be midafternoon before she got there.

But he was living near there. He had to be. Farlane McFarlane. She would have him before nightfall. Then she would just have to sit on him and wait out the last two days until Liam McGillicuddy came to meet her.

Just two more days. Then surely she'd leave this place forever. It would fade from her memory even as Prairie Springs was already doing, lost in the cloud of dust kicked up by the rover's treads. She would be gone before the dust could even settle.

4

THE TOWN of Flat Valley was much farther north than Scout had ever been. As the rover rolled on, the hills around her grew ever taller. She could even see the dark smudge of mountains on the horizon. The rover crested the top of a sprawling ridge that extended out from the hills to the east, slowly fading down to the level of the prairie to the west. Far to the north was another similar ridge, the two like the arms of a prostrate worshiper spread as far as they could reach into the prairie, fingers splayed wide into its red-gold grasses. Between the arms was bare mud and rock dotted with sparse scrub, the typical ground covering in the hill country. She could almost smell it, the sharp sage-like aroma the scrub gave off when stepped on.

And in the center of that scrubby plain was the town, even smaller than Prairie Springs. It had no metal wall, nothing to catch and reflect back the sunlight. From this distance, it looked like nothing more than a strange rock formation standing far apart from the rest of the hills. But the rover map was labeling it Flat Valley.

Once the rover was down the ridge and back on level ground, Scout got up to stretch her back and then went down the steps to check on the dogs.

Shadow raised his head from where he had curled up at the bottom of the stairs, tail wagging somewhat uncertainly. Scout bent to give him a pat on the head and a little scratch behind the ears.

Gert was sprawled across the center of the floor and stirred not at all.

Scout's eyes fell on the pistol lying on the table in the dining nook. Her stomach clenched, and she felt like she had eaten mud and it was hardening in her belly.

She had threatened a bunch of kids. She had never intended to shoot them, but then she hadn't intended to draw the weapon either. Who was she now that she had so little control over her impulses?

She was prepared to live with the nightmares from what happened those four days underground, for the rest of her life if she had to, but she vowed she wasn't going to let that fear change her.

Neither was she going to become like those assassin girls who had killed most of the others during those long four days. Once they had been the same as her, perhaps, but then they had changed. They had gone to living beyond fear, beyond any feeling, willing to do anything at all. That couldn't be her either.

She remembered Gertrude: always calm, always in charge. She had to find a way to become like that. Even when she was afraid for her life.

Scout left the pistol on the table and went back into the rover's cockpit, all too aware of the different weight to the belt now that the holster at the small of her back was empty.

She could see the town more clearly now. Unlike other towns, the buildings here had never been parts of containers dropped from space. They were made from blocks of stone stacked into walls that were a bit on the short side. Slabs of plastic molded to look like wood were stacked to form the roofs of the buildings. Scout had seen plastic like that used for tabletops. It was pretty durable for that use. Never having seen actual wood, she had no idea how convincing the illusion was, but such tables were common in the cities.

But she had never seen those tabletops used for roofing. It might keep out the glare of the daylight sun or the occasional sprinkling of rain, but it had to be useless against an ejection storm. What did these people do when the alarms went off?

Scout's hand on the seat back trembled as a horrible image floated up in her mind. The whole town dead, nothing in those buildings but radiation-burned bodies huddled together.

But that wasn't possible. Someone had answered Ruby's call. They had seen the man she was looking for. They must have a safe place to wait out the storms.

The rover rolled to a halt a respectable distance away from the buildings and Scout dropped back down to the rover's main floor. The dogs both looked up at her this time.

"Come on, dogs," she said as she pushed the button to open the door. Even that little gesture made her breath hitch with sudden pain. "We're sticking together this time."

There couldn't be more than twenty or so inhabitants here, not enough of a population to support any street kids, but Scout wasn't taking any chances. Shadow jumped up and down, ecstatic to be going out with her. Gert yawned sleepily, but her tail was wagging, too.

The dogs ran off into the scrub the minute they were outside. Scout stayed by the rover, waiting for the door to seal shut again before stepping away.

The dogs came running back to her when she whistled with tails wagging, bodies crouching and bouncing, trying to entice her to join them in the scrubby grass to hunt for smells or the occasional small animal. But when she turned to walk into town, they quickly fell into step beside her.

The town consisted of four smaller buildings skirting a larger central one. That had to be the public house. She could see no signs of people anywhere, but the doors to the four smaller structures, also of plastic molded to look like wood, were all shut. The public house had larger double doors, the plastic slabs flat against the sides of the stone walls like shutters thrown wide open to let in the wind and the sun.

Scout stopped in the doorway to let her eyes adjust to the light inside. The roof was even less adequate as shelter than she had supposed, little shards of sunlight penetrating between slabs in scores of places, covering the dirt floor with golden circles like coins of light. The floor was otherwise bare, but tables and chairs were stacked on the wall to Scout's left as if someone was planning to host a dance.

"Stranger," a woman's voice said out of the darkness at the far end of the room. It was easily the oddest greeting Scout had ever heard.

"Yes," Scout admitted. "I've come from Prairie Valley. I'm looking for someone."

"Ruby sent you," the voice said.

"She did," Scout said. She took another step inside the building but still couldn't spot the speaker.

"Your dogs are welcome here," the woman said.

Scout looked back at Shadow and Gert. They were both standing at the threshold, as if waiting for permission to enter. That was somewhat odd from Shadow, who occasionally waited for guidance from Scout but rarely obeyed others. It was very odd from Gert.

"Come, dogs," Scout said, and the two charged past her. Gert immediately disappeared in the gloom on the far side of the room, but Shadow's white coat glowed all ghostly. He jumped up, putting his paws on something.

Scout squinted until at last her eyes could pick out the form of an older woman, stooped with sparse wisps of white hair floating around her sun-darkened scalp. Scout stepped closer. The woman looked anything but frail; the hands offering some sort of treat to each dog may have been gnarled with age, but the arms were still all hard muscle.

"I was looking for someone," Scout said.

"I've seen him," the woman said. "Not lately, not with the storm. He didn't shelter with us, but then he generally keeps to himself."

"Where do you shelter?" Scout asked.

"You're standing on it," she said. Scout looked down to see a hatch under her feet. More molded plastic, already half-covered with dirt from the floor, although the townspeople would have just come up out of there this morning.

"This plastic is enough protection?" Scout asked.

"That's just the drop down to the cave mouth," the woman said. Gert was pawing her, and she bent down to give the dog another treat and rub around her ears. She spoke to the dog in a singsong: "We go ever so much deeper than that, don't we, darling? To a cavern so large it has its own lake. A whole other world just a kilometer under your four paws. I bet you'd like it down there, wouldn't you, darling? Play fetch in the lake, chase cave rodents. Wouldn't you?"

Scout looked down but, of course, saw nothing but the toes of her own dusty boots. A natural cavern with an underground lake? That she would love to see. A shame she was on a job. And after that, she would be leaving this world forever.

"Do you know where I can find him? Or start looking for him, anyway?" Scout asked.

The hard edge returned to the woman's tone now that she was talking to Scout and not the dogs. "If you step outside and look to the east, you'll see a hill that's lighter in color than the others. Head that way. That's where he walks in from."

"So he could be anywhere in that direction?" Scout asked. She tried to keep the whiny undertone out of her voice—she hated herself whenever she heard it—but there was no hiding that she was disappointed. This was going to be much harder than she thought. And she only had three days.

"If there's one thing we like less than strangers in these parts, it's strangers snooping into other people's business," the woman said sharply. "I'm telling you this much because Ruby tells me it's important."

"It is," Scout said. "Thank you."

She started to turn to the door, but then turned back as a dark thought stabbed into her brain.

"He's not from here," she said. "Like really, not from here."

"Not my business," the woman said. Her voice was still unfriendly, but she smiled down at the dogs. Scout was glad she had brought them with. She hadn't wanted to leave them alone, but now they were clearly also helping her keep this woman talking when otherwise she likely would have stalked away minutes ago.

"Has he been here long enough to know to take shelter from a coronal mass ejection?" Scout asked.

"If he has any sense, he knows that," the woman snapped. "I don't go mothering others for free."

Scout nodded and said no more. She wondered what the odds were that her mission was going to end with her standing over a radiation-burned body after all. "Thanks for the help," she said, then whistled for the dogs. She was half afraid they would ignore her, preferring the company of the treat-dispensing woman, but they both ran to join her as she stepped back out into the stiflingly hot day.

She had to drive the rover manually now, having no destination to program into the navigation system. But she could lock down the steering and speed controls long enough to stand up and get a brief look around now and again.

The rover's narrow window defined the horizon, framing the hills before her in a panorama. She half expected to see one hill shining brighter than the others based on that woman's description. At first glance, they all looked alike, blending into each other in the glare from the afternoon sun.

Then, as the rover continued rolling across the flat plain, she began to see differences. The farthest hills were bare rock with a blasted and twisted look, as if they had once been mountains before becoming victims of some indescribable violence. The middle-range hills were more of what she was used to: red clay with sparse grasses and shrubs of sage green.

But one hill closer to her than all the others was gray. It seemed a featureless gray at first, as if by some optical illusion it appeared closer than it really was, smudged by the distance like the mountains to the north. After nearly an hour of rolling over the sunbaked earth of the plain, she started to see a bit of texture. Another hour and she was certain that this hill, unlike all the others, was covered in gravel. Or was entirely made of gravel. An enormous mound of gravel left out here in the middle of nowhere. But who would do such a thing, and why?

The baked earth here was as smooth as the streets in the domed cities. It was almost as if they were gliding in a hover car. But she knew the rover treads were not as silent as a hover car. She had to find this man's hideout, to have eyes on it before they drew near to it. Otherwise, when he heard them coming, he could flee, and she'd never know what direction he had fled to.

At last she saw something: a low hut built entirely from slabs of the plastic molded to look like wood. Where had all the plastic slabs in this region come from? This hut was even smaller than the stone structures in Flat Valley. It was more the size of a child's fort. If a man lived in there, he never got off his knees unless he went outside.

There was no sign of motion. The ridges were taller and closer together here, the sound of the rover's motor echoing back and forth between the two rock faces.

Either she had missed seeing him flee, or he hadn't been here in the first place.

Or he was still inside.

Scout parked the rover outside the hut, then clambered down the stairs.

She looked again at the pistol on the table. She felt like it was looking back at her, judging her, taunting her. In the end, she snatched it up. Too many people had told her to be careful. Leaving it behind when she might need it would be very foolish, perhaps fatally so.

Reaching behind her to slip it back in its holster sent another stab of pain through her chest. She was unlikely to forget the events of that morning, even if she found herself in danger again, not with that pain always ready to remind her.

Scout hopped outside, and the dogs jumped down after her. She expected them to run off into the sparse grass again, but they stayed close at her sides. Shadow was sniffing the air, the hair on his back bristling tensely, and Gert kept swinging her head from side to side as if searching for something.

Scout stepped up to the hut's open doorway. It faced the sunset, and she stood just to one side to let the sun light the interior. She squinted as details became apparent to her eyes. The floor of the hut was a meter down from the doorway, dug down into the packed earth with no steps to reach it. She could only make out the bare ground just below the doorway. Scout squatted, still keeping to one side of the door so as not to block the sun, and pushed her hat off her head to lean around the doorframe and peer inside.

She jumped at the sight of a man inside, staring back up at her as he lay sprawled across the floor.

"Damn," Scout said. "Too late." For he was quite dead.

The dogs sniffed at the doorway but had no interest in going inside.

They went around to the back of the hut, snuffling at the ground and occasionally catching each other's attention so they could both sniff at the same fascinating scent.

Scout jumped down to the floor of the hut, never taking her eyes off the man. He remained motionless, definitely dead, but not from the storm. In fact, she would guess he had died after the storm, the blood around the bullet wound in his chest just starting to dry and turn brown at the edges.

Someone had beaten her to her prey. But who? He was a stranger on this world, and while she had no doubt he had many enemies all across the galaxy, none of them knew he was here. So who had shot him, and why?

"Did you know him?"

Scout spun at the words—from a boy speaking in a conversational tone—and realized belatedly that once more the pistol had found its way into her hand.

5

SCOUT FORCED herself to keep the pistol steady. She shouldn't have drawn it, but now that it was out, putting it away would be a mistake, and looking like she was afraid of it would be even worse. The sweat that had poured off her when she had been outside was chilling her in the coolness of the hut that snuggled half in the earth. The shivers that she fought against, that she couldn't let betray her by making the gun barrel tremble, were as much from the sudden cold as from nerves, but he wouldn't know that.

Whoever he was.

He was standing in the doorway, blocking the setting sun, the outline of his body glowing with a golden aura. By his size, he was about her age, and he appeared to be wearing a loose-fitting shirt over closely fitted pants, but more than that, she couldn't tell. He didn't seem to have anything in his hands, but one rested on the doorframe, blending with the shadow. Anything could be hidden in that hand.

Scout swallowed and looked around in quick glances, building a picture of her surroundings. The diffuse light that escaped around him lit up the tiny hut as if it were already the gloaming, everything color-less but with defined outlines. A low table, completely bare save for water circles like the ghosts of steaming mugs past. The round indentation in the ground where the man must have sat at that table, wearing away at the earth under his buttocks a little each time. One long shelf dug into the opposite wall containing a stack of MREs, three canteens, and an electronic tablet that, while not as fancy as Gertrude's, was also definitely not a local make. A bedroll spread in the far corner.

The body sprawled half across the bedroll.

The hut around her felt too small, and when she shifted her foot, it bumped up against the body, like there wasn't room enough for both of them. He hadn't been dead for long—blood was still running from his body to be soaked up by the filthy bedroll beneath him—but the air was already full of a metallic tang that clung unpleasantly to the back of Scout's tongue even when she breathed through her nose.

She was getting far too familiar with that smell. Congealing blood.

"Hey now," the person in the doorway said again. "No need for the gun. It was just a question. I wasn't accusing you of anything."

"What are you doing here?" Scout demanded, not lowering the weapon.

"I could ask you the same," he said.

"I'm asking the questions," she said.

"Because you have the gun?" he asked.

Scout remained as she was for a moment, then tucked the gun away in its holster. Although his tone had been of someone unbothered with being in a gun's sights, she saw his posture relax a bit after she had put it away. But she kept her hands near her hips as she had seen Gertrude do on so many occasions.

Not that she had Gertrude's swift drawing reflexes. But then he didn't know that.

She still couldn't see him through the halo of light that glowed around him. She couldn't see his eyes or even his face to judge whether he was trustworthy or not.

But she had never been one for lying or even hiding the truth. No reason to change that now, even after everything that had happened. None of that would have ended any differently, no matter what *she* had done.

"My name is Scout Shannon," she said at last. "This man ripped someone off. I'm here to bring him in on behalf of a friend of mine. Too late, apparently."

"Bring him in where?" he asked.

"Never mind," Scout said. "Your turn."

The outline of a boy squatted, then dropped down to the hut floor. He brushed invisible dust from his palms as he straightened. Scout took half a step back, not out of fear but to get out of the blinding glare of the setting sun, which he was no longer blocking. She stopped in the corner where the shelf ended, the back of her right hand brushing against the neat row of canteens.

She could see him now. His age was hard to guess. He sounded about her age, but his skin was sun damaged enough to make his face look older—not bad yet, but deeply tanned, with creases forming around his gray eyes. Not unexpected, given his lack of hat or sun-protective shirt that Scout had. She doubted he had any of the sunscreen she so carefully rationed out for herself.

He must spend a great deal of time outdoors. His loose shirt had once been white, the jeans beneath it once blue, but both were fading into the same dusty earth color. He had a vest on over the shirt, the kind with dozens of pockets, although from the way it hung around his body, those were all empty. His hair was jet black but neatly trimmed; as far as they were from proper civilization, the trappings of civilization at least weren't unknown to him.

"I'm Tucker Hawke," he said, extending a hand to her. She wiped her hand down the thigh of her cargo shorts before taking his in a brisk shake. "I'm afraid this fellow has ripped off many people. I was on my way here to talk to him on behalf of just such a person when I heard your rover pull up. You found him like this?"

"Yes," Scout said. "I just got here, but he's been dead for a couple of hours, at least."

Tucker leaned over the body, then looked up at her. Something about the way his gray eyes regarded her through thick, dark lashes made her stomach flutter most annoyingly. "How do you know?" he asked.

Scout reminded her stomach that it was most definitely not in charge and resisted the urge to soften her hard tone when she answered. "The blood is browning over here on his shirt and the bedroll, but it's still wet over here," she said, pointing. "He must have been in some sort of shelter during the storm or he'd be showing extensive radiation damage. So someone came all the way out here and shot him this afternoon."

Tucker gave a low whistle. "Well, he had enemies."

"You're from this area?" Scout asked. She kept her tone conversational, but her eyes took in every detail of his body. The pockets of his vest were definitely empty. His pants had no pockets at all, and he was wearing canvas shoes with no visible socks. There was a large, blank screen strapped to his left wrist.

He had nowhere she could see to hide a gun.

Tucker tipped his head to one side and gave a noncommittal shrug. "Near here, but I come out this way a bit." He looked around the room, picking up the tablet and turning it over in his hands before setting it back on the shelf. "I've never been in here before. Rather empty, isn't it? He must keep his contraband somewhere else. I would say under the floorboards, but, well..." He lifted a sneakered foot to look at the bare earth underneath.

"This is disappointing," Scout said, still looking down at the body. Farlane McFarlane was looking less and less like the picture on Gertrude's tablet every moment. His skin was turning ashen and the features of his face almost seemed to be caving in.

"Also smelly," Tucker said. "I'm going back outside."

"Yeah," Scout said, but as he climbed back out of the hut, she stayed behind, putting the lens over her left eye and taking a little camera from Gertrude's belt. She recorded the scene from every possible angle, then sent the images to the tablet.

But then she paused, tablet in hand. She had wanted to prove herself useful to Liam. She wasn't sure finding a dead body would do that, but that's all she had now. She just had to tell him what she'd found and wait for his response.

Tucker wasn't wrong about the smell. Scout drifted closer to the doorway and the fresher sage smell from the scrubby grass as her thumbs ran over the keyboard only she could see on Gertrude's tablet.

She only had time for a brief note letting Liam know she had found the culprit, but had found him dead.

She sent the message and tucked the tablet away, but stopped again before climbing out of the hut. The man's personal tablet might have information on it, perhaps more incriminating than what Gertrude had already acquired. Maybe financial records extensive enough to restore the stolen funds to the proper owners. Maybe a long shot—he certainly didn't seem to be living like a rich man now—but Scout saw no reason not to be sure. She took the tablet off the shelf and put it in one of the large exterior pockets on the side of her cargo shorts.

"Um, Scout?" Tucker called. He spoke lightly, but she heard an undertone of barely contained fear beneath it. She fought the urge to draw her weapon again.

"Trouble?" Scout asked, poking her head out of the hut. He was nowhere in sight. She bit her lip at the stab of pain in her chest as she pulled herself up and out into the outdoors.

"Potentially," he said, and she followed the sound of his voice to find him perched on the hut's plastic roof, pulling himself higher and drawing his feet in as close as he could to get them away from the ledge. "There's a vicious animal out here. Um, make that two vicious animals."

Scout climbed out of the hut. She could hear the sound of Gert growling, low and fearsome. Shadow must be just a touch farther away, his less-fierce growl lost beneath the sounds emanating from Gert.

"Come, dogs," Scout said, slapping the side of her thigh. Shadow came at once. Gert put her paws up on the edge of the hut to peer up at Tucker, who had ascended to the highest point. "Gert!" she commanded and slapped her thigh again. Gert dropped to the ground and came to Scout, but not without a great deal of whining.

"Oh," Tucker said. "*Your* vicious animals."

"Yes," Scout said. "You can come down now. They won't harm you unless I ask them to."

Tucker slid down but remained a respectful distance away from her and her dogs. "I'm not sure that's entirely comforting."

"No, it shouldn't be," Scout said.

A sudden feeling of emptiness rolled over her. This mission had been the only thing she had to fill the time while she waited to be picked up and taken away forever. Without it, she had nothing of any importance to do. She could keep the rover rolling, catch up on more sleep, maybe teach Gert a few basic commands.

But she didn't think it would be enough. Not for the rest of today and for two more whole days. Not enough to keep the emptiness from filling up with other feelings.

She needed to keep moving, to stay busy, but how?

"You okay?" Tucker asked, taking a step closer but stopping again at Gert's warning growl.

"Yeah," Scout said, but she doubted that sounded any more convincing in his ears than it did in hers. "Where I waited out the storm, it was a bit of a nightmare."

"Close quarters?" Tucker asked, but when she didn't answer, he carried on. "It was for me. Seven of us without enough room to lie flat, all our legs overlapping. We could sit across from each other with our backs against the walls, but that makes for awkward sleeping. I still haven't stretched out the kink in my back." He held his arms up high, then out wide, then straight back, but he gave up with a sad shake of his head. "Maybe tomorrow. It was a long one, though, right?"

"Too long," Scout said. "They're getting longer. And more frequent."

"Ah," Tucker said, and she shot him a quizzical look. "You're one of those conspiracy types. The evil machinations of the Space Farers at work." He wiggled his fingers like a street performer overselling a children's story.

"I'm not a conspiracy type," Scout said, resisting the urge to touch the data disks in her pocket. She knew they were still there; they were always digging just a bit into her thigh. "They are getting longer and more frequent. That's a fact."

"Could be solar changes," Tucker said.

Scout said nothing. He was watching her too closely, studying her face as he waited for her to speak again. She didn't like the scrutiny, especially as she had no clue what answer he expected or what expression he was watching for that would betray her. Instead, she turned to look back at the rover still standing alone in the scrubby grass.

"I should probably just get going," Scout said. "It will be dark soon. I don't know what actual vicious animals might be lurking, waiting for the cover of darkness to pounce."

"Quite sensible," Tucker said. If he noticed her teasing by mentioning vicious animals, he didn't react to it.

"Yeah," Scout said again, looking at Tucker, then back at the rover, then back at Tucker again. "Well, goodbye." She wanted to add a "see you," but that would be too dishonest. She was never going to see him again.

"Hey," Tucker said, taking another quickly aborted step closer to her, reaching out a hand to catch a sleeve that was far out of his reach. Scout stopped and looked back at him. "It is going to be dark soon, sooner than I can get back to my place."

"You walked out here, you said?" Scout asked. There was no sign of another vehicle anywhere around the hut, not even a bicycle, and yet the ridges to the north and south were very far away, with nothing between but sparse scrub and that weird mound of gravel.

"Yeah," Tucker said. "Can I trouble you for a lift? It's not far." Scout frowned, but he raised his hands, showing once more that he was harmless. "I get that you don't want to be bothered. But it's really not very far at all, and I can offer you a hot dinner on the other side."

"I have a kitchenette in my rover," Scout said.

"This is fresh food cooked over an open fire. Proper food. Come on, who says no to that?"

Scout frowned again. She didn't know who would. She was afraid it wasn't going to be her.

"Hold out your hands to my dogs," she said. Tucker looked first confused, then a bit frightened. She could clearly see him gulping as he steeled his will and extended a palm to each dog. Scout had never met anyone so afraid of her animals. His eyes kept moving from one dog to the next, taking quick glances in between at Scout to see if she was still calmly watching.

Shadow gave a brief sniff, then started licking the offered palm with almost embarrassing gusto. Gert approached more slowly, but after her own olfactory inspection she sprawled out on the ground at Tucker's feet, offering her belly up for rubs.

"Get up, Gert," Scout said sharply. "Don't be so eager to please." Gert rolled back up, tail wagging as she watched Scout approach. Tucker held up his free hand in case Scout wanted to sniff him as well.

"Do I pass the test?" he asked.

"You pass *a* test," Scout said. "I'll take you back to your place. We'll see about the food later. I might stay. Or not."

"Totally up to you," Tucker promised. "It's just east of here, a little farther into the hills."

"Don't you mean up?" Scout asked as she slapped a palm on the lock to open the rover door.

"No, no," Tucker said. "I mean in. You'll see."

6

SCOUT LIFTED BOTH DOGS INSIDE, then waited for Tucker to climb up before closing the door. He lingered in the alcove that housed the door, eyes sweeping over the room. Scout felt a stab of self-consciousness at the general untidiness of the space. The crates full of broken or disassembled appliances, the liberal sprinkling of random tools all over the place—that had been Ottilie, but the mess in the kitchenette was on Scout.

"It's not mine, I'm just borrowing it," Scout said. She couldn't keep herself from sweeping the empty MRE containers into the recycler and tossing the sporks into the sink.

"Oh. It looks like you live here," Tucker said, looking toward the bunks in the back. The top bunk was overflowing with more boxes of junk, but the bottom bunk contained nothing but bedding sloppily arranged into a nest that no longer held an old cat.

"Just for a few days," Scout said. "Help yourself to whatever you can find in the kitchen if you like. I'm going to get us rolling."

"Thanks," Tucker said and opened the mini-fridge to peer inside.

Scout climbed up into the rover's cockpit, the dogs close at her heels. There was a brief altercation as they fought for space on the passenger seat, scuffling and barking that ended with a loud yip from

Shadow. Gert barked back her deep, booming bark, a frightening sound that would surely seem to mean she won any argument, but she hopped down to the floor of the cockpit, curling up with her head just touching the side of Scout's boot. Shadow sat up in the seat that was now entirely his, his back straight and his head high with an air of magnanimously *not* rubbing in his victory.

"All settled?" Scout asked, then grabbed the wheel and started the rover rolling in a lazy circle until the hills were directly in front of her.

Then she saw that the rover's path was going to pass close by the gravel mound and her curiosity was piqued once more.

"Do you know what this thing is?" she called down to the back of the rover. Tucker came to the top of the steps, a glass of water in his hands. The sides were already beaded and running with moisture and Scout's mouth felt suddenly parched just looking at it. He had filled the largest of the glasses. And that was not water from the recycler; it was almost half of the fresh glacial water Ebba had left in the fridge.

"No," Tucker said, squinting out the window. "Slag from a mine? But I don't know of any mines near here. It's always been there, so far as I know."

"You've always lived around here?" Scout asked.

"Just for the last five years or so," he said. "Do you see the gap in the two hills up ahead? Aim for that gap. It's going to become a canyon. Might be a bit tight for your rover, but nothing you can't handle."

Scout said nothing. The hours of that day represented the sum total of her driving experience, but if she looked competent to him, she was scarcely going to correct his faulty assumption.

"Have you felt any earthquakes here lately?" Scout asked.

"Earthquakes?" Tucker repeated with a frown. "Isn't that more of a coastal thing?"

"Usually," Scout admitted with a sigh. What *had* happened that morning? Some freak of her imagination?

"Why do you ask?"

"Forget it," Scout said with a wave of her hand. He watched her drive for several minutes while she tried to ignore the feeling of those gray eyes on her.

"So, what's your story?" he asked at last, taking another sip of water and moving to sit on the edge of the passenger seat. Shadow and Gert were clearly still making him nervous, and Shadow was prepared to defend his perch on the seat. Scout reached past Tucker and put a hand under the dog's rear, lifting until he gave in and hopped down to the floor. Tucker sat down but kept his feet in the aisle between the seats, nowhere near the deeply napping Gert.

"My story?" Scout repeated, looking over every panel around her and trying to seem busy. She couldn't look at him for more than a bit at a time without her stomach flopping over again. Stupid stomach.

"You're not from here," he prompted.

"I make deliveries and carry messages," she said. "Usually on my bike, but this rover was temporarily left in my possession."

"Where do you live, though?"

"Nowhere," Scout said.

"Where's your family?"

Scout bit her lip before she could snap back "at the bottom of a crater." He wasn't trying to upset her. "No family. Not these days. Not for ages."

"Just two wild dogs?"

"They're not wild. Shadow—that's the white one—he's actually quite highly trained. Gert is still a puppy, though."

"This big black beast is still a puppy?" Tucker said, eying the dog sleeping near his feet.

"Yeah," Scout said. She wasn't sure exactly how old Gert really was. She had just been there one morning when Scout and Shadow woke up, curled up against Scout's feet with no intention of ever leaving them. She had been about Shadow's size then, but with enormous paws she still hadn't quite grown into. Her puppy days might be ending, but she was far from exhibiting adult dog behavior.

To Shadow's frequent annoyance.

"You don't like to talk about yourself," Tucker guessed.

"No more than most people," Scout said.

"A lot less than most people, actually."

"I guess I wouldn't know," she said, annoyed. She didn't like feeling judged. But he seemed unperturbed by the edge of anger in her voice.

"I guess someone with your nomadic lifestyle probably gets to meet all sorts of people, but you never stay in one place long enough to really get to know them."

Scout didn't reply. They had reached the valley between the hills, and as the canyon walls closed around the sides of the rover, she no longer had to pretend to need to give all her attention to driving.

"Since you're clearly not going to ask, I'll just tell you about myself," Tucker said, taking another sip of the glacial water. "I also am without family. My parents and brothers were killed four years ago when the Space Farers dropped their rocks from orbit. I was staying with an uncle at the time, sort of a punishment for a school infraction. He was supposed to 'turn my attitude around.' He had a hut on a hill overlooking the city, close enough to get inside the gates if the coronal mass ejection event alarms sounded. But of course there were no alarms that day, no warning. And I saw it all happen from up on that hillside. I saw the meteor streak across the sky. It looked so small and seemed to move so slowly that I could reach out a hand and stop it. But of course I couldn't."

He paused to take a drink, although whether he was truly thirsty or just anxious to let the thickness in his voice pass before speaking again, Scout wasn't sure. Her throat felt tight as well. She remembered that day. Four rocks had fallen through the atmosphere to hit the four largest cities, sparing the capital. She hadn't seen the one that had taken out her home, but the impact of it had sent her tumbling off her bike from kilometers away.

"Which city?" Scout asked at last.

"Sunshine Valley," he said.

"Me too," Scout said, her voice barely more than a whisper.

His face lit up. "Your family was there too?"

"My parents, and my baby brother. All gone now. I only had Shadow with me."

"I'm so sorry."

"Me too. I mean, I'm sorry for your loss," Scout said. The canyon was still very narrow, but it ran straight long enough for her to risk a glance over at him. His gray eyes were shining a bit too brightly, and he quickly looked away.

"There can't be many of us out here. Survivors of Sunshine Valley, I mean. Quite a coincidence we should run into each other like that."

"You have no idea," Scout said under her breath. She didn't want to reveal that she hoped her remaining time on the planet was short. She didn't want to jinx it. But she couldn't help thinking, another few days and they would never have met at all.

"Maybe we knew each other?" Tucker said, the jaunty tone back in his voice. "We look about the same age. Seventeen?"

"Sixteen," Scout said.

"Close enough. What part of the city were you in?"

"It was a big city," Scout said, certain the odds were slim that they had been close. "My parents were bakers. We lived at the edge of the western market."

"Ooh," Tucker said with a wince. "We were in the south quadrant, near the gate. My mother was a gate guard. My father taught at the high school. History."

"And you had brothers, you said?"

"Yes, two. Both older. Both home that day."

"But you still have your uncle?"

"Alas," he said with clearly artificial good cheer, "he died less than a year after the strike. It broke his heart, I think. He was an eccentric; only my father really understood him. He was never the same after. Then he caught a strain of flu that was going around and just couldn't shake it."

"So you've been on your own ever since?"

"Yes, but I found some people who took me in. We're nearly at their doorstep now," he said, straightening up in the seat to look out the window. "It's going to get tight at this next turn, but on the other side, it widens out again. This is the last tricky bit."

"Okay," Scout said, clutching the controls as she worked the pedals, guiding the rover on its treads through a canyon with walls curved tight around them like a tunnel dug by a worm. The top corners of the rover's body were grinding against the rock, sending a cascade of grit and dust raining down on them.

The rover jammed, briefly, then lurched forward, rocking so hard it woke both the dogs from their naps. Then they were out in a wider canyon.

With the sun so low in the sky, the light reaching them had a scattered quality, muting the colors of the world around them. Scout was used to this effect near sunset. So when the colors of the canyon walls around her snatched her breath away, it left a deeper ache to know what this place would look like in the full light of day.

The walls of the canyon were like rainbows, band after band of bright color, but not in layers like sediment. It was as if someone had painted diagonal stripes of indigo, peridot, ruby, topaz, jade, amethyst, and a thousand more. The canyon floor was the same red clay she knew from all over the hills, but she had never seen anything remotely like this before.

And the canyon walls were not just high—more than twice the height of the rover—they were also nearly completely sheer. The only way to get out of this canyon was back the way they had come. It was like a magically secluded space. She was so grateful she had gotten the chance to see it before she left this world behind.

"I've never even heard of this place," Scout breathed.

"Aren't you glad you agreed to drop me off?" Tucker asked with a smile.

Suddenly both the dogs sat up at once, hair on their backs standing tall as they went on high alert. Then Scout heard it too, the roar of engines echoing and reverberating off the canyon walls.

"Where is that coming from?" Scout asked, trying to stand up without taking her feet off the pedals. The rover was meant to be piloted by someone a bit taller than she was, but more importantly by someone with a copilot to stand and keep a 360-degree watch out the vertically narrow but panoramic windows.

"Behind us," Tucker said, turning to look out the back window. He was about to say more, but his words were lost in the sudden outbreak of barking. Shadow's bark was alarming enough, but Gert's deeper growling woof was terrifying, even for Scout. She woofed again, and the blood drained from Tucker's face. He dropped the glass onto the seat, sending water everywhere. He turned paler still and tried to climb up onto the backs of the two seats.

"Relax," Scout said, reaching behind her head to push his foot away. His toe was digging into the back of her neck. "They aren't going to hurt you. Tell me who's outside. Welcoming party?" Scout asked him. The roar of engines was all around them now. The canyon's acoustics were twisty, but Scout was certain she should see what was practically on top of them. The rover had cameras in various places, but none of the screens were showing anything, not even a stirring of dust.

"Please call your dogs off," Tucker said.

Scout glanced over to see the dogs jumping up at where Tucker was now pressing himself between the passenger seat back and the roof of the cockpit. He had impressive acrobatic abilities, but his unusual behavior was too puzzling to the dogs. Ironically, his fear of them was leading them to see him as a threat.

Shadow jumped again, snagging the hem of Tucker's pants and pulling.

"Shadow, down!" Scout commanded, but the dog knew he only had half her attention as she once more stood up on the pedals, trying to see out the narrow windows.

The engines sounded huge, but what if they were actually little? Little but noisy?

"Are these your friends?" she asked again.

"This dog is trying to kill me!"

Scout glanced back again and saw Gert standing on the seat, her massive paws digging into Tucker's hip. Gert was still growling, but she was watching Tucker closely, as if expecting him to do something to explain himself.

"If you get down from there, they'll calm down," Scout said.

"I don't think I can." If it was possible for someone to sound like they were about to faint, that was how he sounded. She could barely even hear him over the continued barking and the roar from outside.

Scout stopped the rover and stood up on her own seat, pressing her face tight against the thick glass.

Down below, a three-wheeled motorcycle was pacing the rover right next to the forward treads. The bike was covered with armored plating, and a long gun barrel ran along either side of the rider. The rider was wearing a body-concealing long white duster, face hidden behind helmet and goggles. She could barely tell if it was human or not. Then she realized the rider was using some sort of tool to remove the bolts from the rover's treads. She didn't bother looking out the other window. With two dogs and a boy between her and a view out that side of the cockpit, it wasn't worth the effort, but she was certain she would see another, similar figure engaged in the same activity on the other side.

She glanced down at the monitors. Yep, they had busted out the cameras that were trained on the treads.

Scout dropped back down into the driver's seat and pressed down on the accelerator, all the way to the floor.

Whoever these people were, they weren't going to take her down so easily. The rover roared down the canyon, rattling as it went. Occasionally, she heard the ping of something breaking free.

Just how much damage had they done in that minute she'd parked to look around?

The rattling became a grinding, but Scout kept on, leaning her whole weight in to keep the pedal flat on the floor. Because, past the grinding, she could hear the whine of their engines in pursuit.

She was not going to go down easy.

7

SCOUT CLENCHED HER JAW, focusing on keeping the rover steady at full speed as the treads under them started shaking apart. She was vaguely aware of the canyon walls rushing past them on either side, drawing ever closer as the canyon narrowed. The rattling that echoed through the cockpit was louder than the still-barking dogs. She could feel it in her teeth; they would be chattering against each other violently if she loosened her tight hold on her jaw for even an instant.

There was a slight metallic tang on her tongue. At some point she'd bitten down on something but didn't give it the attention to figure out if it was lip, cheek, or tip of her tongue. Instead, she narrowed her eyes, not letting the rover jump to the side as it propelled out of another dip in the ground. Her arms were aching already. She'd be losing this battle with the control yoke soon.

"Isn't there a hatch in the roof of this thing?" Tucker asked, pounding a fist against the metal hull.

"The dogs won't hurt you!" Scout snapped.

"It's not the dogs. I need to get outside and signal to the others before they plant the incendiary devices. They aren't responding to my messages."

"Before they what?" She longed for a stretch of clear ground so she could look back at him.

"Stop the rover," Tucker said.

"These are your friends?" Scout asked.

"Yes. Just stop. I'll open the back door so they can see me. But hold on to your dogs."

Scout slammed down on the brakes, acutely aware of the sound of loose bits from the treads rattling loose, raining down on the baked earth of the canyon floor.

"I asked before. Why didn't you answer me?" Scout asked, turning to glare at him the moment the rover had stopped rolling.

"I—" But he broke off, glancing at Shadow and Gert as if they were waiting to jump him if he said a word against them. "I told them we were coming, but I guess they weren't checking their messages. A lapse of protocol." He tried to shoot her another smile, but it quickly died. "Just hold on to your dogs." Then he vaulted down the steps to the main compartment of the rover.

"I don't like orders," Scout said. She got up from the driver's seat and stood at the top of the steps, blocking the dogs behind her. Shadow pressed his snout between her calf and the rover wall, snuffling loudly. Gert was whining and pawing at the back of Scout's thigh hard enough to hurt.

"Sorry, but there's a time factor," Tucker said, looking around to find the controls for the door. He pushed the button, then stepped back as it emerged from its recess in the wall of the rover and swung open with a clang.

Tucker jumped out of the rover and quickly moved out of view. Scout glanced back at the monitor screens behind her, but several had gone dead, the exterior cameras they linked to now smashed.

"Stay, dogs," she said as she moved slowly down the steps and past the dining area to stand in the open doorway.

Tucker was standing alone a few meters away, shading his eyes against what remained of the setting sun. It was no more than a red slash on the horizon now, the first stars already awake and twinkling brightly in the east. The canyon walls now appeared to be only a diagonally banded gray. Scout narrowed her eyes until she too saw the dark shapes moving toward them out of the setting sun.

She had left the rover running, the engine echoing loudly here where the canyon was so narrow, but the sounds of the approaching engines quickly drowned it out. Shadow pressed up against her calf, trembling. He had no love of loud mechanical noises, especially ones that never seemed to end.

Gert was less bothered, and Scout had to reach down and catch her collar before she could jump out of the rover and run to investigate. Scout wanted her dogs near her, inside the rover, just in case she needed to slam the door shut and make her escape. Or at least hunker down in what safety the rover's thick hull provided.

Tucker raised an arm and waved it back and forth twice. The dark shapes slowly gained form as they approached, becoming ghostly white, flapping figures astride monstrous vehicles like armored dinosaurs. They raced up to Tucker, drawing close enough to make Scout wince, although he just waited calmly as they slammed to a halt on either side of him. A cloud of reddish dust enveloped newcomers and Tucker both.

Gert whined, tugging a bit at the collar still in Scout's grasp.

"Hush, girl," Scout said, waiting for the dust to settle. Before it had, the last sliver of the sun slipped below the horizon, taking all its light with it. Scout glanced up at the moonless sky. The stars were bright enough to give the basic details of the world inside the canyon, like a rough pencil sketch, but she needed more than that. She looked at the controls by the door and found one to turn on the exterior lights.

The light was far brighter than she had expected, like the sort of light they used at spaceports to guide in the craft with faulty navigation equipment. Tucker turned back to glare at her, but she wasn't sorry.

The shapes made more sense now in the full light. The wispy ghosts were people dressed in long white dusters to protect from the glare of the sun. They had been driving with hoods up and held in place by the goggles that now dangled around their necks. The skin around their eyes was clean, almost pale against the reddish dust that coated their lower faces and foreheads.

Teenagers, Scout realized, like Tucker and herself. The boy with close-shaved dark hair was leaning in to speak close to Tucker's ear. The girl stood a bit apart, listening but not speaking. She reminded Scout a bit of Ottilie. Ottilie had worked on the crew of one of the big guns the Planet Dwellers had used to fire into space during the war. This girl was built much the same: tall, wide shoulders, massive fore-arms. But where Ottilie had kept her silver hair buzzed short, this girl had a sloppy braid of ash-blonde hair wrapped around her head like a crown.

"These are your friends?" Scout asked, pitching her voice to carry over the meters of empty ground between them. Tucker didn't respond at first, still listening to the boy speaking in his ear, occasionally nodding but more often scowling and giving little shakes of his head. He kept tapping the little screen on his wrist demonstratively.

As the boys argued, the girl raised a hand in greeting to Scout and Scout hesitantly returned the gesture.

The other boy finished talking with an overly elaborate shrug of his shoulders and turned back to climb back aboard his armored motorcy-cle. The two massive gun barrels ran down either side of the bike, starting at a mechanism that spanned the back of the seat, a belt of ammunition running in and out of a box just behind the rear wheel. The barrels thrust out awkwardly to either side of the front wheel.

"Those must be hard to aim," Scout said as Tucker walked back to the rover. He gave her a questioning look, then glanced back as the girl turned her bike to follow the boy.

"It just takes a bit of practice," Tucker said.

"What's going on? If these are your friends, frankly, I'd rather you hopped a ride with them and let me be on my way," Scout said.

"You're going to need repairs," Tucker said. He was looking under the rover as he spoke, examining the treads. Scout hopped down to get a closer look herself, and the dogs jumped down after her.

"I wouldn't need repairs if you would have said sooner that these were your friends. Or if you had told them we were coming." The damage wasn't as bad as she had expected. The treads were still running on their tracks, but barely, and a lot of bolts were missing. She saw a few in the dust behind the rover, but it would be impossible to find them all in the dark, sprawled out across the length of the canyon as they were.

"Yeah, I did try to tell them. And it was no good you slowing down before they knew you weren't the enemy. I really thought there was a hatch up there… sorry," Tucker finished, giving her a lopsided smile of apology as he rubbed at the back of his neck. Scout didn't return the smile. "I am sorry. But Bente and Ken will have you fixed up in no time, I promise."

"How much time is 'no time'?" Scout asked, picking up the bolts she could see gleaming dully in the starlight.

"Leave those. We have plenty back at the base. And Bente and Ken can have you fixed up just after dinner. I did promise you dinner." He tried another smile, but Scout still didn't respond in kind.

"I didn't accept that offer," she said.

"Oh, yeah?" he said as if he hadn't remembered that, but his tone wasn't convincing. "It's going to be fine, I promise. You'll get something to eat, and afterward you can go on your merry way. You and your dogs," he added, looking down at the two still standing close at her sides. He tried his smile on them. They were unmoved as well.

"I don't really have a choice, do I?" Scout said.

"Hey, don't be like that," Tucker said. "You're going to like the others."

"How many others?" Scout asked, liking each new development less than the last.

"It depends on who's home and who's out on missions," Tucker said with a shrug. "But I promise we'll stuff you so full of the best food you've ever tasted that you won't want to leave. Especially since it's already after dark. You might as well wait for morning to move on."

"I don't want to wait," Scout said. She was standing closer to the door than he was. She could scoop up Gert and get inside—Shadow could make the leap on his own—then slam the door and just drive away. Leave him behind in her dust.

Only she was pretty sure he wasn't lying about the damage to the rover.

"That's fine," Tucker said, raising his hands as if surrendering. "You want to leave right after dinner, that's fine. Bente will have you all fixed up by then. She's a whiz."

"Bente, that was the girl out there just now?" Scout asked.

"Yes, that was Bente. And Ken. They were on patrol."

"Patrolling for what?" Scout asked.

"This close to the hills, this far from the cities, there are lots of bad folk hiding out here. Like McFarlane dead back in his hut and whoever killed him. Only these others are quite alive, and they tend to travel in groups." He glanced past her out the open door of the rover. "That light is like a beacon, you know. We really should get to safety. It's not safe out here at night."

Scout bit her lip as she considered the situation. She didn't like trusting people she had just met. She almost laughed out loud, a darkly self-mocking laugh, at that thought. If she had learned anything over the last four days she had spent trapped underground waiting out the solar storm with strangers, it was Never Trust Strangers.

Still, she couldn't fix the rover on her own. She had crossed the hills many times on her bike, but farther south, where the hills were the turf of only the rebels, and they kept themselves hidden. She didn't know if Tucker was telling the truth about the dangers of this part of the world. He could be lying to lure her into some sort of trap.

Or he could be telling the truth. Because, having just met, what reason could he have for trapping her? If he just wanted to rob her, he could have done that while she was in the hut and her rover had been standing unattended several meters away.

Scout crossed her arms and gave him an assessing look. There was only one question that really mattered. Did he have a reason to lie to her? But she had no way to answer it. And she could scarcely ask him.

She had no facts. All she had was her gut instinct.

"All right," Scout said at last, and Tucker let out a whoosh of held breath and tried yet one more weak smile. "I'm not happy about this. If you had said something before they destroyed my rover treads, I wouldn't be in this mess. I don't like feeling like I've been manipulated away from making my own choices."

"I understand," he said solemnly. "I didn't mean for that to happen.

I did message them before we got to the canyon. And after that... well, I'm not used to dogs."

Scout rolled her eyes.

"I *am* sorry," he persisted. "Can I show you something?" She nodded, then pulled back in alarm as he reached for the fastening on his pants. "Don't worry, it's just my hip," he said, pulling down the waistband on one side. There were marks there, so faint they would be invisible on the sun-damaged skin of his arms, but they contrasted sharply against the pale skin of his hip.

"What is it?" Scout asked.

"Dog bite," he said, fastening his pants back up. "When I was a kid. A really little kid. Like, two? It's my earliest memory. I literally remember nothing else until I was like six. But that memory, of the dog coming out of nowhere to knock me down and then sinking its teeth into my hip..." He gave himself a little shake. "My mother had to chase after that dog to get me back. I was sick for a long time after; I guess one of its teeth chipped my bone or something. I don't remember that part so well. But being under that dog, its breath on my face, the inescapable largeness of it? That I can never forget."

"I'm sorry. I didn't know," Scout said. "My dogs are good dogs."

"No doubt," Tucker said earnestly. "That dog was a stray, probably starving, with no better options. But you guys are cool, right?" He put his hands out to the dogs again and they drew closer to lick at him. He looked up at Scout through his lashes and her stomach did that flip-flop again.

"They seem to like you," Scout said. She kept the steely tone in her voice, although all of her anger was floating away from her. "You're sure we can roll this thing to where we're going with all the damage?"

"Sure," he said briskly. "Just keep it at a slow, non-jangling roll. Bente and Ken will let the others know we're on the way. Shall we?"

Scout stayed as she was, arms crossed protectively over her chest, even though it made the bruise throb, for another beat, but then she relented and hoisted Gert into the rover.

She really hoped she wasn't going to regret this.

8

SCOUT HAD NOT YET ATTEMPTED DRIVING in the dark, but once she had turned off the floodlight over the door, she found that the monitors still attached to working cameras compensated for the low light, showing greenish outlines around the protrusions in the canyon walls and the occasional larger rock embedded in the baked mud of the ground. She got the rover moving as slowly as she could, a bit herky-jerky at first but smoother once she found a switch that automated the speed and let her take her foot off the pedal.

Tucker let the dogs curl up together in the passenger seat, leaning against the console between the two control panels and watching her as she navigated down the canyon.

"Which way?" Scout asked.

"Just keep going like you are," Tucker said, not even looking at the monitors. She nodded, hoping her cheeks weren't coloring. Those gray eyes watching her so closely were more than a little disconcerting.

"Until when?" Scout asked.

"It will be obvious."

Scout nodded again. She wondered if there was a polite, nondefensive-sounding way to ask someone to stop looking at you.

Then he leaned forward and pushed her hat back off her head. She was sitting forward in the seat—she had to in order to reach the pedals —and the hat fell down her back to hang from its string around her neck.

"Hey," Scout said, but the canyon was narrowing again and she couldn't spare a hand from the controls to replace her hat.

"I just wanted a better look at you," he said.

"What for? Put my hat back before I crash us into a wall."

"Yes, ma'am," he said, lifting the hat off her back, then brushing the blonde curls back from her face before setting the battered old hat back on her head. She had showered that morning before blowing up the compound, a rare treat. But she had been sweating on and off most of the day and those curls had been first soaked and then dried into crusty curlicues against her skin. She was acutely embarrassed he had even touched them.

Well, he was a sweaty mess himself. And yet his hair floated in a perfect wave, spilling over his forehead. Was he vain about it? Was that why he wore no hat? Because that decision wasn't doing his skin any favors.

She fought the urge to heave a sigh. Premature wrinkling aside, he was nearly as cute as he thought he was, smiling at her all the time.

"Do you see it yet?" he asked, startling her out of her thoughts. Then she looked back at the monitors and saw what he meant. The rover systems were having a hard time defining it, but the greenish outlines ahead of her were slowly coalescing into a sort of gate.

"I think so. That's where we're headed?"

"Yes. They left the door open for us or you'd never see it at all," Tucker said.

Scout watched the rover system fight to find the outlines of that gate. The canyon wall extended up out of sight on all sides of it.

What a perfect place for a trap.

Scout switched back to manual speed control and let the rover roll to a halt. Tucker looked at her quizzically.

"What are you?" Scout asked.

"What do you mean?"

"Look, I just spent the last four days locked in a secret place no one could find from the surface, and while I was down there, I watched nine people die, one after another."

"I'm sorry. That must have been horrible," he said with what sounded like genuine empathy, but Scout didn't let it melt her anger.

"I'm not going to repeat it. I'm not going into another super-secret location with no facts."

"Fair enough," Tucker said. "But most of it isn't my secret to tell. I can promise you'll be safe, and as soon as the repairs are done, you will be free to go."

"I have no reason to believe you're trustworthy or that your promises mean anything," Scout said.

"I guess not," he allowed, tugging at his bottom lip while he stewed in thought. Scout slumped back in her seat, arms crossed as she waited for him to go on. At last he just shrugged. "I've got nothing. I can probably persuade the others to let Bente come out here and fix your rover for you while you wait. In the dark. She can lug her tools this far; she's strong."

"Don't try to guilt me," Scout said. "You're the reason I'm even in this mess. I should have left you to walk back on your own after I found you."

"I *am* sorry," he said, reaching out to grasp her shoulder but thinking better of it at her hard glare. He let his hand fall. "Look, it sounds like you were just through a truly terrible experience and it's left some scars. Totally understandable. I went through some nasty stuff myself those first few years on my own after my uncle died. Not that bad, but bad. Then these people found me and took me in, and they've been taking care of me ever since. Now I'm in a position to do some of that caring myself. Clearly, I'm not very good at it yet. But these people are my family. Maybe the thing you need the most right now is to sit at a proper table, filling your belly with warm food, surrounded by warm people."

Scout felt herself relenting. She didn't like it.

"Give us a chance to show you not all strangers are bad. I mean, most are," he quickly amended with a grin. "That's why Ken and Bente did what they did. We don't like strangers any more than you do. But I feel like I already know you well enough to know you're our kind of people. And if you give me a chance, I can show you that we're your kind of people, too."

"Fine," Scout said. "But mainly because I don't want Bente to have to haul a bunch of tools out here and work in the dark, okay?"

"Of course," Tucker said. "Just keep rolling straight in."

Scout uncrossed her arms and sat forward to get the rover moving again. She thought she heard Tucker blow out a sigh of relief, but when she looked up at him, he just flashed that too-confident smile at her again.

She didn't return it.

The monitors still had a hard time pinning down exactly where the green outlines of the gate were, but it was wide enough that Scout could navigate between the innermost versions of the shifting outlines with room to spare on either side. Once the nose of the rover was through the gate, they were bathed in floodlights even brighter than the light over the rover door, shining down from some point higher up the canyon walls. Even through the window, Scout could make out no details; the lights blinded her so that all she saw beyond them was black. Were they in a nook off the canyon with sky still above or was she once more underground in an immense cavern? She couldn't tell; the lights were too bright to see stars even if they had been there.

The ground here was the same as the ground outside the gate, packed down mud that might have been wet once decades ago but was now slowly eroding away into dust that whipped around in eddies as the rover treads stirred it up. She saw the armored bikes parked off to the right of the gateway, next to a small four-wheeled vehicle. It might have been a jeep or a dune buggy; it was hard to tell what was going on past the bristles of armaments and all the metal plating.

"Do you get into many battles?" Scout asked, only half-jokingly.

"It's best to be prepared," Tucker said. He was standing now, one hand on the back of her seat as he looked out the narrow window. Ken and Bente were in front of the rover now, guiding her in past an array of lights set on the ground, blinding her from seeing the deeper expanse of the cavern or canyon or wherever they were. First Bente and then Ken put both hands up, palms out, and Scout braked the rover. Bente gave her two thumbs up, which Ken quickly echoed, and Scout killed the engine.

"I guess you're home," Scout said.

"Come on," Tucker said, suddenly energized. "I can't wait to introduce you to everyone."

He leapt down the steps to the main compartment of the rover, the vigorous movement setting the dogs to barking as they charged after him, but they were just excited. Scout hurried after to be sure he didn't recoil in fear again, but he seemed to be managing better now, laughing a bit as the dogs jumped all over him, desperate for his attention. He gave her a half grin with just a little nervousness in his eyes, but the dogs were oblivious.

"They think you're taking them out to play," Scout said. "You might want to walk calmer."

"They can run through the open parts of the compound all they like," Tucker said.

"I'd prefer they stayed close to me," Scout said.

"Of course," he said, still overeager to put her at ease. She opened the door and waved her arm for Tucker to go out first.

Ken and Bente were waiting outside. They had taken off their long duster coats, although Bente still had her goggles dangling around her neck. They both wore the same fitted jumpsuits underneath, with belts as bulky with equipment as the one Scout wore around her own hips. Ken had cleaned up already, even his hair glistening wetly as it stood straight up off his scalp. Bente was still wiping the dust off her face and neck with a cloth.

Tucker turned to hold out a hand, but Scout leapt down without assistance. The dogs hopped down after her. The air here was cold enough to raise goose bumps all over her flesh. It wasn't just the usual cool that descended after sunset. This was a bone-deep cold, like this place never baked in the light of the sun. *Was* it a cave?

Shadow found a scent he wanted to follow and raced off, but Gert pressed close against Scout's leg, trembling, and Scout put her hand on the dog's head to calm her. She had no fear of machines, but people made her nervous.

"Ken, Bente, this is Scout," Tucker said. "She picked me up outside of McFarlane's hut."

"Oh, yeah?" Ken said, giving Tucker a darting little look before extending a hand to Scout. "Welcome."

"Am I?" Scout asked, but shook his hand, anyway. Ken gave Tucker another look and Tucker made the smallest of head shakes.

"Yeah, sorry about that," Ken said and flushed with pretty convincing chagrin. "We missed his message."

"And you're Bente?" Scout said, turning to the girl. She was even larger up close, fairly looming over Scout, although she seemed shy about shaking hands. But when she did take Scout's hand, it was a warm, comforting squeeze, more like a fond hug than a token gesture.

"I better close the gates before Joelle—" Ken started to say, but his words were quickly drowned out by a voice coming from beyond those blinding lights.

"What is going on here?"

"Shit," Ken mumbled under his breath. Bente hunched her shoulders as if trying to make herself smaller, less visible. Ken shot Tucker another look before scurrying away back toward the gate.

"Joelle," Tucker said, but the voice cut him off again.

"Save it, Tucker." Her form eclipsed one of the floodlights, growing more defined until she at last became visible. She was shorter than Scout but wore her hair pulled up tight on the top of her head, where it puffed out in a thick mass of dark, glossy, tight curls that made her seem taller. Her skin was deeply brown but unmarred by the sun damage that lined Tucker's face. There was a roundness to her cheeks and the curve of her eyebrows that Scout would normally equate with friendliness, but clearly at this moment Joelle was livid. She wasn't wearing a jumpsuit like Ken and Bente, but the tight pants and tank top she wore under her tactical vest had a look almost like a military uniform. She had a screen strapped to her wrist identical to Tucker's.

She stopped in front of Scout, arms folded as she looked the newcomer up and down. Scout fought the urge to take off her hat and hold it in front of her like she was being chastised. Gert cowered further behind Scout's legs. Shadow was hiding behind the rover tread.

It would have been a more effective hiding place if his fur didn't glow so brightly even in the shadows.

"Why," Joelle said, not a question. She directed the word at Tucker without ever taking her eyes off Scout.

"I messaged you. Surely you got it."

She gave a curt nod, her eyes unblinking.

"Then I've already explained. It just seemed like the thing to do," Tucker said.

"My father—"

"Will understand when I talk to him," Tucker interrupted, making her eyes narrow. "Where is he?"

"Still out," Joelle said.

"I don't know what this is about," Scout said. "Your friends have damaged my rover. Tucker promised repairs. Then I'll be on my way."

Joelle tipped her head to look past Scout at the rover. Then she seemed to notice the dogs for the first time.

"It was entirely my fault, and I'll make the repairs myself if Bente has other work," Tucker said.

"Oh, stop it," Joelle said. "You can't fix a child's toy, let alone this rover."

"I promised to make this right," Tucker said. "And dinner. I also promised dinner."

"I have food," Scout said. Retreating with her dogs to the comfort of the rover interior was feeling like a better option all the time.

"No, no," Joelle said, finally relenting. "I'm sorry. Some protocols were breached here, but clearly that's not *your* fault. We have more than enough to share. I probably made too much, anyway. First night out of the storm shelter, sick to death of packaged food, you know?"

Scout nodded, but, in fact, the bulk of the food she ate was packaged food. She had occasionally splurged on fresh soup or stew if the public house where she was staying had something particularly tempting on offer. But the range she traveled on her bike seldom strayed out of the southwest quadrant, where grain was nearly the only food grown. Fruits and vegetables, those were more of a northeastern thing and usually quite out of her price range.

She was suddenly curious just what dinner would be.

"Dogs," a boy's voice said.

Joelle had been about to speak, but turned to look past the lights behind her. This voice was small, hesitant. A young boy, not yet a teenager. The last of the anger had melted from Joelle's face when she turned back to Scout. Now she looked a bit worried.

"Are your dogs good with kids?" she asked.

Scout had a sudden flashback to that morning, another pang of regret. "When the kids are good with them," she said.

Joelle looked at Gert, still pressed tight to Scout's legs, then at Shadow, taking the first tentative steps out from under the rover.

"They look scared," Joelle said. The worry on her face intensified a notch. She had good reason; scared animals could react in violent ways. But Scout was certain that Shadow wouldn't harm a fly, and Gert had been mightily provoked before she had resorted to biting.

"I'll keep an eye on them, but they should be fine. They've just had a long day," Scout said, suddenly feeling all the hours of it herself. She was tired.

"I've never seen a dog," the boy said as he appeared out of the light. He had the same dark skin as Joelle, the same warm brown eyes, although his hair was cut close to his scalp like Ken's. He had the lanky look of someone who had just shot up a lot of centimeters in a short amount of time, his ankles and wrists protruding from his too-small clothes. He put out his hands and waited for the dogs to approach him. "I've read about dogs," he went on. "Man's best friend."

"They're certainly my best friends," Scout said, gently encouraging Gert to follow Shadow in investigating the boy.

"This is Reggie, my little brother," Joelle said. Scout would guess the kid was about twelve.

"I'm Scout," she told both of them. Reggie dropped down to one knee as the dogs sniffed him all over.

"Do your dogs know any tricks?" Reggie asked.

"Shadow knows a few," she said.

"Is this one Shadow?" Reggie asked.

"No, that's Gert," Scout said. "The white one's Shadow. When he was a puppy, he followed me everywhere, and my dad said he was my little shadow. The name stuck."

"Hey Shadow, Gert," Reggie said, carefully moving from light touches to full-on head scratches. Scout wondered what he had read about dogs. It appeared to have been quite thorough. He knew just how to put them at ease. It might end up being a good thing that they had stopped here, that the dogs were getting a good experience with a kid so soon after their bad experience with kids. She didn't want them getting fearful or mean.

"Can we eat?" Tucker asked, pressing his palms together as he waited for Joelle to answer.

"Might as well," Joelle said. "Come on, Reg."

Reggie had sprawled down on the ground, letting both the dogs nose him all over, tails wagging madly, but he leapt to his feet to follow his sister, the dogs trailing close at his heels.

Well, they had certainly made a new friend quickly.

Scout was about to follow when a loud metallic clang suddenly echoed through the space. Scout flinched, afraid to look back.

"That's just the gate closing," Tucker told her, but she found that not the least bit reassuring. "There are other doors out. Smaller, people-sized ones," he went on. Her anxiety must be showing if he was trying to reassure her. "As soon as the rover is fixed, we'll open the door back up and let you out. You understand we can't just leave it open, not even at night. *Especially* not at night."

"Of course," Scout said, but she couldn't help looking back even as she followed the others toward the blinding floodlights.

The doors behind the rover were firmly shut, some sort of massive wheel locking the two together. There was a mechanism, a machine that would control that lock. There had to be. No human could turn that wheel with their hands, not even Bente with her arms bigger than most people's thighs.

Scout bit down on her lip and forced herself to turn her back on that gate. She told herself that even if it never opened again, all that was trapped was the rover. She and the dogs could escape any number of ways.

But still, she felt trapped. And she didn't like it.

9

SCOUT BLINKED AS the floodlights all turned off at once, plunging everything around her into darkness. She blinked again, then deliberately kept her eyes open wide, waiting for them to adjust. It didn't take long; the darkness had only seemed absolute compared to that blinding light. She could see squares of light ahead of her that she took for windows and a longer rectangle that must be an open door.

Tucker was waiting for her next to that doorway, leaning on the wall outside the door so that the light within bathed his features. Scout hurried to join him, but even as she walked, she tipped her head back to look up into the darkness over her.

Stars. Not a cavern. The walls around her were tall and sheer, probably unclimbable, although that was difficult to tell by starlight. Still, not enclosed. But narrow enough that the bottom would only get sunlight for maybe an hour near midday, hence the chill. She felt ever so slightly better.

"Your dogs are already inside," Tucker said. "They quite like Reggie."

Scout stopped next to him, just outside the doorway. She could hear the voices of the others within: Reggie laughing, Ken chatting a mile a minute with occasional brief responses from Joelle. She didn't hear Bente. Had she gone in or stayed behind to start the rover repairs?

There was a hiss, like water drops striking metal left out in the noonday sun, then a rush of smell. Scout breathed it in deeply but couldn't identify it. The scent was rich, mouthwatering, and yet completely alien to her.

"Hamburgers," Tucker said, watching her face as she puzzled over the aroma. "Have you ever had hamburgers?"

"You mean like meat in a bun?"

"Please—Joelle has her own recipe that is way beyond just meat in a bun," Tucker said with a wave of his hand. "They're fantastic."

"I've had beef in MREs before," Scout said. "Beef stroganoff, beef chow mein, chipped beef with toast."

"Yeah, I'm not convinced any of that is strictly speaking *beef*," Tucker said with a sly smile. "And such little amounts."

"Even heated up, they never smell like this."

"I know, right?" Tucker agreed. "Now, to be honest, this isn't the best beef either. Still no cows on this planet, not even in the northeastern cities. But this is vat-grown beef, which they tell me is a pretty close approximation."

"I wouldn't know," Scout said.

"Me neither, although someday I will," he said fiercely.

Scout looked up at him. Did he too dream of leaving this world, of seeing the rest of the galaxy?

"Come on," he said. "Let's join the others. We all pitch in on the work around here."

"Of course," Scout said and followed Tucker inside the doorway.

The room beyond was long but narrow, running along the exterior wall that faced out on the open space where all the vehicles were parked. It was lined with equipment, most appearing to be turned off or in sleep mode but others running programs, their screens displaying text Scout couldn't quite read as Tucker took her elbow and guided her through the room.

"Top secret?" she asked.

"Well, it might be okay, but it's not my call," Tucker said.

"Whose call is it? Joelle's?"

"Her dad's," he said. "He's not here now, but he should be back soon. I'm sure he'll have no problem with you seeing anything, but like I said—"

"Not your call," Scout finished. "Not a problem. I'll probably be gone before he even gets back, anyway."

Tucker didn't answer that.

They crossed the room to a hallway of closed doors, although next to each door was a window into what appeared to be a darkened office. Then the hallway ended in a warmly lit room, half covered with the same metal roof that covered the offices and equipment room they had just passed through, the other half open to the starry sky. In the middle of the floor of the open half of the room was a shallow pit covered with grates. Under the grates, flames danced over darkly glowing embers.

"What are you burning?" Scout asked.

"It's a chemical compound that simulates wood fire," Tucker said. "We have a bunch of it in one of the storerooms. It's amazing stuff; I don't know why they don't have it in the cities. Can you smell it? I love that smell."

Scout sniffed again. There was something—a fresh, dry sort of smell—but mostly she still smelled the hamburgers Joelle was tending to on the far side of the fire pit. Scout had only smelled wood once, many years ago, as part of one of her deliveries. Someone had sent a bundle of toys to a friend expecting a child and amid the brightly colored plastic there had been a single wooden unicorn. She sniffed again but couldn't find that smell in the amalgam of scents coming from the fire pit.

"When we're done eating, you'll be able to smell it," Tucker said.

Joelle sat back on her heels, long spatula tipped back but not quite touching her shoulder, like a soldier saluting with a sword. Ken was on the other side of the fire pit setting roll halves sliced side down over a part of the fire that was burning much less vigorously than it was under the beef.

"How's that cheese coming?" Joelle called.

"Nearly there," Reggie said, slicing another square off from a long orange log of cheese and setting it on a plate. The two dogs were right beside him, both sitting at rigid attention. He cut off another slice and Scout could swear he deliberately botched it, cutting unevenly so the square broke off midway through. He broke the piece in half and tossed each dog a bit of cheese. Scout snatched his out of the air, but Gert fumbled with hers, having to retrieve it from the swept earthen floor. She didn't seem to mind the dirt.

"Where do you get all this food?" Scout asked. Her experience with cheese was also entirely from MREs, which, like the beef, was probably some synthetic substance flavored to pass as cheese. She had never even imagined it came in great logs like Reggie was carefully wrapping in cloth to put away.

"Places," Tucker said vaguely.

"Top secret," Scout guessed, and he shrugged.

"Plates," Joelle called without looking up from the grill.

"Follow me," Tucker said, leading Scout to the roofed part of the room. There was a long table here, benches lined up neatly on either side. The far wall was entirely cabinets and drawers of various sizes. Tucker opened one of the larger cabinet doors and handed Scout a stack of plates. "Put those around the table. I'll bring a platter for Joelle."

Scout walked around the long table, putting a plate down at each step. She watched Joelle arranging Reggie's slices of cheese on each of the beef patties. Tucker carried a platter so big that Scout doubted her fingers would touch if she circled her arms around it. He held it out for Ken, who snatched the hot toasted buns off the grate and lined them up on the platter. Then Tucker walked around the end of the fire pit to where Joelle was using the spatula to peek under the burgers.

"Forks too," Reggie said to Scout as he returned from the room he had taken the cheese to, now with a plate covered in an opaque wrap in each hand. He set a plate on each end of the long table and pulled the wrap away, revealing two small mountains of sliced onions, tomatoes, and pickles.

"Where are the forks?" Scout asked.

"Drawer on the end there," he said, pointing vaguely. Scout found it on the second try.

Bente came in through the hallway and headed to a sink set into the back wall. Her hands were already streaked with grease and she scrubbed at them with a little brush, looking repeatedly over her shoulder at Ken until he noticed her. He gave her a thumbs-up and went into the room where Reggie had left the cheese and emerged with a large covered bowl. Scout was just setting down the last of the forks as he unfastened the lid. The bowl contained a lumpy white and yellow mass.

"Potato salad," Ken told her. "Bente's specialty. You're going to love it."

"Mustard?" Scout asked, looking more closely at the streaks of yellow.

"And egg," Ken said.

The others were taking seats around the table, and Tucker tugged at Scout's sleeve until she climbed over the bench to sit down next to him. Reggie sat down next to her, the dogs close behind him in case he had more cheese. Scout watched the others and mimicked their movements, loading up her burger with a rich, red slice of tomato, a thick slice of onion, and a generous stack of pickles. She squeezed a spiral of ketchup and another of mustard, then placed the other half of toasted bun on top of everything and pressed down until the condiments oozed out the sides. Then she took a bite.

Bliss. Only slightly mitigated by the hot juices that stung a bit as they dripped down her chin. She ducked her head over her plate. Tucker handed her a napkin, and she mumbled a thanks around a full mouthful of burger before mopping up her chin.

"What do you think?" Reggie asked. Joelle, who was sitting across from her, paused before taking a second bite of her own burger to see how Scout would answer. Ken looked up from spooning a mountain of potato salad onto his plate. Even Bente's eyes were on her. Scout felt her cheeks flush.

"It's the most amazing thing I've ever had," Scout said through a mouth still half full of beef.

"Told you," Tucker said, taking another large bite of his own burger.

"How come no one else has this?" Scout asked. "Even in the cities, I've never seen it anywhere."

"The governor has it all the time in his mansion," Joelle said.

"You stole this from the governor?" Scout asked after swallowing.

"No, the bandits robbed the governor's supply train," Joelle said blithely. "We just robbed the bandits."

Ken laughed as he handed Joelle the bowl of potato salad. She smiled as she dished herself up a spoonful, then passed it down to Bente.

"Isn't that dangerous?" Scout asked.

"Well, yeah," Joelle admitted. "But we're good at it. We've been doing it for years."

"You guys?" Scout asked, looking up and down the table.

"Not just us," Ken said. "We're sort of the second generation. But this beef here was part of our first solo haul. In case we seem kind of proud of it."

Scout didn't know how to answer that, so she just took another bite of her hamburger. She wasn't sure if it was a taste worth risking her life for, but it came closer than anything else she had ever had, including her hands-down favorite beverage, jolo.

"The bandits steal from the rich," Joelle went on. "We steal from the bandits."

"And give to the poor?" Scout guessed.

"In a way," Joelle said.

Tucker looked like he wanted to say more, but Joelle gave him a little shake of her head and he kept silent, accepting the bowl of potato salad from Bente and putting a large spoonful onto Scout's plate. "Try that," he said instead.

Scout swallowed and took a drink of water to cleanse her palate. No glacier-melt water here, just the usual filtered stuff, but it got the job done. The salad was delightfully cold, creamy, and tangy. Potatoes she had had before, many times, but never like this.

"That's fantastic," Scout said. Bente beamed at her.

"Tell me you're glad I talked you into this," Tucker prompted.

"Okay, I'm glad," Scout relented. "Thanks."

Tucker grinned around a mouthful of burger.

"So this place isn't a town," Scout guessed. "Is it like a family compound?"

"Kind of," Joelle said.

"With a loose definition of family," Tucker said.

"So usually there are adults here too?" Scout asked.

"A few," Joelle said. "Most of them are working on a thing north of here. My father and uncle went out to take care of a different thing. They're on their way back now. You'll get to meet them."

"Okay," Scout said hesitantly. She didn't really mind Joelle's vagueness about everyone's activities. She just wasn't sure she wanted to meet anybody else, particularly not an adult.

"Scout spent the last solar storm underground with some messed-up adults," Tucker said as if reading her mind.

"Not just adults," Scout said. "There were three tweens too."

"You didn't tell me that bit," Tucker said. "Did they get murdered, too?"

"Murdered?" Joelle asked, almost spitting out her drink of water.

"Yeah," Scout said. "But I didn't feel bad about that. They were trained assassins, apparently."

"Girls?" Joelle asked, her voice hard.

"Yeah," Scout said, surprised by the question. Joelle and Ken were both nodding as if this confirmed some suspicion they had. "How did you know?"

"We've been hearing rumors," Joelle said.

"Someone has one implanted in the governor's mansion," Ken added. Joelle glared at him and he gave an apologetic shrug.

"Not anymore," Scout said under her breath. "But wait—you heard this from bandits?"

"Not exactly," Joelle said evasively, but Scout remembered the equipment in the room Tucker had hustled her through. She had seen similar equipment in the underground compound where she had waited out the storm.

"Are you guys in contact with Space Farers?" she asked.

"I wouldn't say contact exactly," Ken said, but he stopped talking at a fierce look from Joelle.

"Never mind," Scout said. "Secrets. I get it. And I really don't want to know."

"No offense," Joelle said.

"No, it's fine. I'm leaving soon, anyway. No need for me to get involved in any of it."

Joelle gave her an assessing look. Scout guessed she passed the test when Joelle took another bite of burger.

"Can I ask one question, though?" Scout asked, caught off guard by her own words. She would swear she really didn't want to know anything about whatever they were up to here, but there was one thing nagging her, one bit of unfinished business left on this, her home world. One last thread she'd like to have neatly snipped before she moved on.

"You can ask," Joelle said. "I don't promise an answer."

"You guys are based here in the hills," Scout said. "I've been over the hills loads of times running deliveries on my bike. I've seen signs of people about, sheltering in caves or leaving tracks on the paths, but I've never seen anyone. Not for sure."

"What's your question?" Joelle asked.

"Have any of you seen any sign of the rebels?" Scout asked.

All their faces fell blank at once and Scout had the sinking feeling that she had just inadvertently breached the most rigid of all protocols. Was she not explaining herself correctly?

"I mean, the rumors say they hide out in the hills, and I've been watching out for them for years. Sometimes I feel like they're watching me when I pass through, but I've never seen anyone. Have you?"

There was another long moment of silence, then all five of them burst into raucous laughter.

"What?" Scout asked, feeling her cheeks heat. "There are no rebels, are there? That's what's funny?"

"Oh, there are rebels," Tucker said, putting an arm around her shoulders to give her a good-natured jostling. "There are most definitely rebels in these here hills."

"Oh," Scout said, slowly understanding. She had spent her whole life searching for the rebels, or more exactly hoping they would come and find her. And just when she had given that quest up, here she was feasting on food plundered from the governor's personal supply train with a quintet of rebels.

Joelle gave her a wink, then tipped her head back to put the last bit of burger in her mouth. The orange glow from the dying embers glinted off of something inside her tactical vest.

Knives. Rows of throwing knives. Ken beside her half rose from the bench to reach for the bowl of potato salad and Scout saw what she had neglected to look for before: the gun tucked in a holster at his hip. His outfit matched Bente's so completely she was certain Bente had one, too. She looked at Reggie beside her. Even little Reggie had a knife on his belt. It looked like a utility blade, but that didn't comfort Scout much.

Tucker squeezed her close to his side briefly, then took his arm off her shoulders to help himself to a second burger. Scout wouldn't consider that gesture so much a hug as a way of letting her know about the pistol he wore tucked into his pants.

She had looked. She was certain he hadn't been wearing that when they were in the hut standing over McFarlane's dead body.

But should she be so certain? She wished she had drawn her gun then and searched him. Or would that just have led to a gunfight?

Scout touched her fingertips to where an ache was forming at her temple. Was she sure? She summoned the image back to mind, and the gun wasn't there. But now it was.

"Hey, Scout," Joelle said, reaching across the table to squeeze the hand still clutching a forkful of potato salad. "It's okay. We're all on the same side here, right?"

"Right," Scout said and mustered a smile. "Definitely. All on the same side."

Tucker's gray eyes were looking over at her through the fringe of his lashes again, but this time her stomach just quaked with nausea.

She had to get out of here.

10

SCOUT HAD INTENDED to excuse herself at the first possible opportunity, but halfway through the second burger Tucker had talked her into, her eyelids started to droop. It had been an epically long day, and the combination of a full tummy and the warmth of the nearby fire were wooing her to sleep. If she had been in a chair, she could have slouched against the back of it, but being on a bench as she was, she just sort of slumped down like she was melting in place.

She was technically still awake, but sort of fading in and out of awareness as the others moved around her. They worked together to gather up the dishes and the remaining food. It was hypnotic watching them. No one was giving any orders, they just each knew what needed to be done, picking up and handing things off like pieces of an elaborate clockwork.

Ken was prattling on again. Scout thought he was talking about the repairs that needed to be done on the rover, but she couldn't focus on the words.

She snapped to full alertness when Joelle shrieked. It wasn't a sustained scream, more a yelp of startled surprise, but Scout was instantly on her feet, her right hand on the handle of her gun.

Then she saw what was in front of Joelle. Gert had dropped an impressively fat rat at her feet and was sitting gazing up at Joelle, waiting for praise. She looked a little confused about the shrieking, her tail wagging a little hesitantly, but she still seemed sure that she would be thanked for her contribution at any moment.

Scout took her hand off her gun and ran it over her tired eyes.

"Where did you find that?" Joelle asked Gert. Gert just wagged her tail even harder.

"I'm sure there are plenty more where that came from," Tucker said. "I told you they've been pouring up from below." He picked up the rat by the tail and carried it to the composter. "They aren't so much attracted to our food as fleeing—"

"Yes, of course," Joelle said, cutting him off with a significant look. More secrets.

Scout yawned. "Where's Bente?" she asked, belatedly noting their party was short a member.

"She went to get your rover jacked up," Ken said. "I was about to go help her. Join me?"

"Sure," Scout said, looking around for Shadow.

"If you don't mind, can we let your dogs run about for a bit?" Tucker asked. "They seem like good hunters, and our rodent population could stand a culling."

As if to prove his point, there was a sudden scuttle of dog nails over baked earth floor and Shadow came charging out of the room where they stored the food. He looked around in confusion, having lost whatever he was chasing. Gert went over to investigate, and the two sniffed their way back into the room.

"I can keep an eye on them for a little bit," Reggie offered. "I'd like to watch them hunt."

"All right then," Scout agreed.

"I'll join you in a minute," Tucker said to Scout and Ken. Ken took Scout's elbow to guide her back down that short hallway and, more importantly, to propel her through the equipment room as quickly as possible.

Scout looked back over her shoulder. She had one brief glimpse of Reggie squatting on his heels, watching Shadow try to crawl under a shelving unit he couldn't possibly squeeze under, and of Tucker speaking earnestly to a stern-faced Joelle, then she was back out in the chill air of the outer part of the compound.

"You just loosened some bolts, right? It should be a quick fix?" Scout said as Ken turned the floodlights back on and they walked out to where the rover was parked. Now she could see why the two of them had guided her in so carefully when she had driven through the gate. She had thought it odd at the time, as there was plenty of space to avoid hitting either their bikes or the lights.

But they hadn't been worried she would hit something; rather, they had been navigating her over something that had been covered with the ubiquitous red dust, some sort of jack. The rover was now hoisted a couple of meters off the ground, leaving enough room for Bente to work beneath. Although tall as she was, she still had to stoop.

"You rode it pretty hard," Ken said. "You might have done some damage. But no worries; we'll take a look. No one yet has made a machine that Bente can't fix. I'm more of a software guy, but since Bente strong-armed me into being her assistant, I've been picking up some things. Getting pretty handy."

Bente looked up from where she was crouched over an open box of tools and gave Scout a little smile. Then she found what she needed and retreated once more to the shadows between the rover treads. Ken was running his hands along the rover exterior, inspecting for damage beyond what they had done themselves to the treads.

"You broke some cameras," Scout said.

"Yeah, sorry. We don't have spares of those," Ken said. He looked back at her. "We did think you were the enemy."

"I know," Scout said and let the matter drop. She'd be gone soon anyway, and the cameras she needed to drive were all still operational.

Bente went back into the shadows under the rover. Ken peered into the toolbox, selected a tool, and started tightening something still attached to the tread mechanism. Bente slid over a box of extra bolts and Ken gave her a nod of thanks without stopping his motion.

"So this place is the hidden rebel hideout?" Scout asked as she watched. She had figured out at least two things in the time she had spent here: that Bente never spoke and that Ken said too much. If she kept her tone casual, conversational, he might just tell her everything.

"One of them," Ken said. "This place was a mining concern back in the day, but I guess they ran out of whatever they were digging for. I don't know, it was abandoned for decades until Joelle's father and Bente's uncle moved in when they were, like, our age."

"How many of you are there?"

Ken looked up, his arm still working the ratchet that tightened the bolt, and gave her an apologetic grin. So he did have limits to what he would say. She grinned back, not wanting to seem like she was probing him for information, even though that was exactly what she was doing.

"I get it," she said. "You can't tell me. But aren't you looking for more recruits?"

"Are you looking to be recruited?" Ken countered, looking her over as if to size up her potential.

"No," Scout said almost wistfully. A week ago, that had been her fondest wish. But so much had changed in just a few days. "This just seems like a small operation for a group hoping to overthrow two different governments, and one of those out of reach up in space."

Ken stopped ratcheting and looked around, as if seeing the compound with new eyes. "We do okay," he said, resuming his work.

"I'm asking too many questions," Scout said.

Ken shrugged, then moved on to the next bolt. "Perfectly understandable. I had a lot of questions too when I first got here."

"Tucker and I are both orphans. Is that the same for the rest of you, too? I mean, I guess not for Joelle and Reggie."

"Right, Joelle and Reggie still have their dad. He runs things here," Ken said. "Their mom was a rebel, too. She was in one of the cities the day the sky fell."

"Doing rebel work?" Scout asked.

"Actually, just visiting her family. Bad timing." He gave her an exaggerated grimace, then went back to the box of bolts and grabbed several more before returning to the tread. "Now Bente doesn't talk about her family outside of her uncle," Ken said. "He's out with Joelle's dad right now. You'll meet them both when they get here, I suppose. Bente came here around the same time I did. Her mother was Arvid's sister, but that's all I know about it. Something must have happened to her mother, but she doesn't like to talk about it. I don't even know if she has a dad or siblings or anything else."

Scout nodded in understanding. It seemed an odd distinction to make, that Bente didn't like to talk about her childhood or family. Bente didn't seem to talk about anything. But Scout kept her attention on Ken. "And you?"

"Runaway," Ken said. "I left home… four years ago?" He stopped working again and his eyes rolled up and to the side as he counted back. "Yeah, four years. Wow. Seems like longer. Or else just yesterday."

"Yeah," said Scout, who had similar feelings about the time since her family had died.

"I was living in the alleys of the capital city."

"That's tough," Scout said.

He looked up at her and arched one eyebrow.

"I deliver messages and packages by bike," she explained. "I avoided the capital, but when I had to go, I always made sure to have a place to stay. How did you avoid the nightly street sweeps?"

"At first, I didn't," Ken said. "I was put in juvenile detention about a dozen times. The city patrols are vigilant about catching homeless kids and locking them up, as it seems you know, but the guards at the lockups are far laxer. It's super easy to escape, especially for a kid with skills like me."

"I've never heard of anyone escaping before," Scout said. "Although I guess the kids I talked to about what it was like inside, they must have gotten out somehow."

"Most get sent back to their families and run away again," Ken said. "Some that escape use that story for cover."

"That makes sense," Scout said. "Is it as bad as they say? Inside?"

Ken stopped working again, raising and lowering the hand that held the ratchet tool as if testing its weight. "It can be," he said. "The worst is that it's so random. There is no way to follow the rules and avoid punishment. It's impossible. The rules keep changing, and some of the guards just like breaking kids."

This time, when he turned back to his work, Scout noticed a silver line meandering across the back of his head, visible through the close-cut black hair. A scar. From what? Those days in lockup?

He would probably talk about it if she asked, but some stories she'd rather not know. "Did you ever think about going back and busting the others out?" Scout asked instead. "Fresh recruits for the rebellion?"

"We don't really have the sort of operation that requires lots of manpower," Ken said, but he flushed when Bente shot him a furious glance. Apparently, he had just said too much again. Scout moved closer as if to inspect Ken's work. She wanted to know what sort of operation they did have. What exactly did they do besides steal and fight bandits? She was about to speak again when they were interrupted.

"How's it going?" Tucker asked as he sauntered into view. He directed his question at Ken, but his eyes were on Scout. She stepped back from Ken. With those bright lights, it was impossible to know how long Tucker had lingered in the dark, watching her firing questions at Ken.

"Should be done pretty quickly here," Ken said, glancing at Bente, who nodded her agreement. "This has got to be the oldest rover I've ever seen—I can't believe it's still rolling and not in a museum—but it's been lovingly maintained."

"Nearly done, good. I really should get going," Scout said.

"At this hour?" Ken asked, looking from her to Tucker.

"I have someplace to be," Scout said. She, too, looked at Tucker. "You promised. Dinner, repairs, then I was free to go."

"I did, but—"

"It's not happening," Joelle said, her voice echoing through the canyon before she even appeared from between the floodlights. "No one is leaving. Not tonight."

11

NO ONE MOVED for a long moment. Bente had just packed up the tools in their box and was about to carry them away, the massive container Scout doubted she herself could lift with both arms dangling easily from one hand as she turned to look back at Joelle. Tucker was scowling and rubbing the back of his neck. Ken looked confused, but tried to muster a friendly smile when he saw Scout looking at him.

Joelle had stopped as soon as they could see her, standing with her arms crossed and a don't-mess-with-me look on her face.

Scout was quite prepared to mess with her.

But before she could speak, she heard the sound of running sneakered feet and many dog nails scratching rapidly over the hard earth. Reggie appeared from between the lights behind his sister, the dogs close at his heels.

Scout felt a momentary stab of jealousy at how quickly her dogs were bonding with this kid, but it melted away when first Shadow and then Gert spotted her and they both charged forward to jump all over her. They had suddenly found her gone, and judging from how furiously their tails were wagging now, they had assumed the worst.

"Calm down, you guys," Scout said, but they kept jumping until she dropped to her knees to hug them both at her sides. The movement made her chest hurt. She was going to have to take a look at that spot where her ribs met her sternum before she went to bed. As tender as it felt, she was sure it must be very purplish black.

"Gert caught four more rats," Reggie told her. "And Shadow got five, so they're tied."

"That's a lot of rats for one evening," Scout said.

"She tosses them up like they're toys, but have you ever seen him shake a rat?" Reggie asked, his eyes wide.

"I have indeed," Scout said. "And things bigger than rats." Then she looked up at Joelle. "So what do you mean, it's not happening?"

"It wouldn't be safe," Joelle said. "Not for us—we never open the gates when we see movement in the canyon on our sensors. Certainly not for you. Armored as this rover is, the bandits can penetrate it in a heartbeat."

"But there's nothing worth stealing inside of it," Scout said.

"Believe me, that will just make them angrier after they fight their way inside," Joelle said.

Scout let go of her dogs and stood back up. Tucker was watching her with that same earnest look in his gray eyes he always had, like he really wanted her to just accept everything so they could go on to being friends or whatever. Joelle, standing with her arms crossed, didn't seem to care whether Scout believed her or not. The gate wasn't going to be opened either way.

"Can I see this sensor movement?" Scout asked.

"No," Joelle said. The stern look on her face said she was never going to bend.

"It's just until morning," Tucker said to Scout. "The repairs are done now. As soon as the sun's up, you can go."

"I can go?" Scout repeated. Joelle, expression unchanging, nodded. "I guess there's nothing more to be said, then."

"You won't leave without saying goodbye?" Reggie asked. "You have to come wake me up. I don't get up real early usually, but I want to say goodbye to the dogs. Promise?"

"We'll say goodbye," Scout promised. She didn't think that would be a hard promise to keep. She'd have to wake someone up to let her out, after all.

"We have extra beds," Tucker said, pointing back over his shoulder with one thumb. He seemed to be indicating a second floor over the one she had seen.

"No thanks," Scout said. "The dogs and I are used to sleeping in the rover."

Which was a complete lie. They had never slept in there. But she knew she'd feel safer with the door shut firmly between her and everyone else, even this crew that were more than strangers and yet still less than friends.

"Okay. Sleep tight, then," Tucker said. "I'll see you in the morning."

She told herself to ignore the obvious disappointment in his voice. She would be leaving in a few days anyway, right? Now was not the time for trying to make new friends. Particularly not these friends.

"You too," Scout said as coolly as she could manage and gathered Shadow up in her arms to set him inside the rover. Gert tried to follow, but although her front paws could reach the bottom of the doorway, her back legs lacked the strength to get herself up and inside. Scout bent and lifted up her back end until she could squirm the rest of the way herself.

"It was good meeting you," Ken said. "Sorry we wrecked your rover, but it was a pleasure to put her back together. She's a cool piece of history; it's a shame she can't stay. Good night."

"Good night," Scout said, then leaned to the left to look around him at Bente, still lingering with that heavy toolbox in hand. "Good night, Bente." Bente blushed and sketched a sort of salute, then turned and walked away. The floodlights kicked off again before she had taken more than a few steps and Scout was once more plunged into darkness.

She climbed up into the rover and shut the door behind her. She found her way to the bunks by touch, then turned on the light in the wall over the pillows of the bottom bunk. The dogs were already there, curled up together at the foot of the bed, noses overlapping. Exhausted from the hunt, she guessed.

And yet she wasn't ready to sleep yet. She took off her sun-protective shirt and let it drop to the floor next to the bunk as she squirmed out of her boots. She hung Gertrude's belt and her father's hat on a hook near the head of the bunk. Then she padded stocking-footed to the little lavatory and pulled down the neckline of her tank top.

Oh yes, a very nice bruise indeed. That would take weeks to even start fading to yellow. She probed it with her fingertips and, as much as it hurt, she didn't think she'd cracked any ribs.

Lucky her.

Scout went back to the bunk, but she still wasn't sleepy. She put Gertrude's eyepiece over her left eye, then pulled the blank tablet from her belt and ran her fingers over the featureless surface where her eye saw buttons.

Liam had gotten her message about the body. His only response was to resend his last message. MEET ME with time and coordinates.

Scout put away the tablet and the eyepiece with shaking hands. Seriously? That was all he had to say? He never answered her questions or acknowledged what she said or did. What was with this guy?

Did she have any chance at all of getting off Amatheon? And what about the data disks hidden deep in her pocket? She was certain the information they contained was dangerous, but to whom? What could she possibly do with them that wouldn't make everything on the surface and up in space infinitely worse?

Scout pulled her knees up to her chest and pressed her forehead against them. It had been a very long day, and the headache that had been fading in and out since she had nearly died of oxygen deprivation days before was stronger than ever. Not to mention the constant ache from her chest. She was exhausted, but she was going to have to calm down before she'd get any sleep. Letting the same unanswerable questions race around her mind in endless loops wasn't going to help anything.

And yet. Why had Tucker been at the con man's house? If he had gotten there on foot (why hadn't he taken one of the motorcycles or the jeep?), he must have started out the moment the storm stopped. What was so important that he had to get there so quickly? And yet, after she had arrived, he had seemed so blasé. The man he had come to see was dead, and he hadn't seemed surprised or frightened or even so much as inconvenienced. Why?

And was there really something dangerous lurking just outside the gate? Was Joelle being honest with her or not?

For that matter, had Ken and Bente actually fixed her rover or only pretended to? She had watched their every move, but she knew nothing about repairing anything more complicated than her own bike.

Scout groaned aloud. She was so tired of questioning everyone's motives from every possible angle, as if her life depended on it. She could never be sure of anything. Better to be prepared for everything.

And the best thing she could do right now was get some sleep. Everything else could wait until morning.

With that thought, she put the tablet back on Gertrude's belt hanging from the hook in easy reach of the bunk. Then she took off her cargo shorts and let them drop to the floor where she had left her boots, socks, and sun-protective shirt. Then she slipped under the sheet and blanket.

Shadow immediately got up and crept to her shoulder, then pawed at her until she lifted the sheet and blanket and let him crawl under to curl up against her belly. Then he settled back to sleep with a soft sigh. Gert sighed as well, putting her head on Scout's ankle and a paw on her foot before drifting back into slumber.

It felt like Scout's eyes had closed only for a minute, but suddenly she was wide awake again, staring into the darkness. Something was moving. Something large.

The gate.

Scout slipped her feet out from under Gert and climbed quietly over Shadow. If they woke, they'd be barking, and she wanted to avoid that. They were tuckered out enough to prefer to go on sleeping, provided she didn't jostle them too much. The two rolled closer to each other to fill in the gap she was leaving behind as she crept away. Good.

She hissed softly when her bare feet hit the cold floor of the rover, but quickly pulled herself up into the top bunk. It was cluttered with crates of loose engine parts and broken electronic devices, but there was just enough room for Scout to snake through to the back wall. There was a small window, low and narrow. She pressed her forehead to the glass as she peered out.

It was still full dark out there, nowhere near sunrise. The gate slowly swung until it was halfway open, then lurched to a halt. The ensuing silence was broken by the soft sound of a motor approaching.

Bandits? Sneaking in with the rebels completely unawares? Somehow, she doubted Joelle was running such a sloppy ship.

Something was definitely approaching, but without light and at this point without a running motor. Scout found the lever that opened the window, only a few centimeters but enough to let in a bit of fresh air and whispers of sound. Her ears could faintly make out a soft grinding: tires over the baked earth of the canyon floor. No engine now, although she had heard one before.

Whoever it was, they didn't want to be seen. They were rolling in, dark and silent. But was it friend or foe?

12

THE JEEP that rolled into view was not as heavily armored as the other vehicles parked in the canyon nook, but the design was similar enough to feel like it belonged here. Scout let out a breath of relief; not bandits. The jeep had no extra guns, but someone had added plating to the exterior, particularly in the front, where it came to a point intended to ram—or more accurately stab—other vehicles.

Scout couldn't make out the driver, but a man in the passenger seat was standing, one hand on the roll bar, looking behind them as they came in the gate. He looked older, with a short ponytail of silvery-white hair and many scars crisscrossing the sun-damaged skin of his massive arms. Some looked like burns, others more like the result of some sort of blade. A warrior's arms. He turned to look forward again and Scout saw eyes the same deep, clear blue as Bente had. He must be her uncle. What was his name? Ken had said it. Right, Arvid.

The moment the jeep was clear, the gate started to close with a low rumble.

"What the heck is that?" Arvid asked, gazing up at the rover.

"Visitor," Joelle said as she walked out of the dimly lit equipment room to the still-rolling jeep. The driver braked the jeep with a lurch and then stood up to climb out of the door. He landed on the ground in front of Joelle. This had to be her father. He towered over her, but their skin was the same deep shade of brown, and her no-nonsense body language and stern facial expression were a miniature of his.

"Visitor?" he repeated.

"Someone Tucker ran into this afternoon," Joelle said.

"Tucker," her father said. "Figures. This isn't the time to be bringing strangers around."

"I know. He had reasons, I guess."

"Tucker was supposed to go see McFarlane," he said with a frown.

"He did. McFarlane is dead."

"Dead? How?" But before Joelle could answer, he took a step closer to her. "Did he get my stuff first?"

Joelle shrugged. "I don't know what happened. He'll tell you, but he won't tell me. He certainly seemed to be empty-handed. Anyway, with our visitor, we've been careful. It's just one girl, and she'll be gone in the morning. I didn't want her leaving at night, maybe drawing attention to us. Since the storm ended, we've been seeing a lot of motion in this area. Some of it is really close to us. I guess the bandits are getting hungry."

"It's not just bandits," her father said. "War is coming. That's starting to become obvious to everyone. It's making people anxious."

"Nah," Arvid said with a shake of his head. "They don't know. It's just the storm. After a doozy like that one, lots of folks are starting to see the benefit of gathering in larger groups with better shelters."

Joelle's father stiffened, his whole body tightening up much like Shadow's did when he saw something he wanted to chase. Or to fight. Apparently Joelle's father didn't like to be contradicted. Arvid, digging in the back of the jeep with his back to the others, didn't notice his reaction, but Joelle did. Scout couldn't see her face well enough to make out any expression, but she took half a step forward and touched her father's arm to get his attention.

"Did you find her?" Joelle asked. She looked past her father to Arvid in the jeep. There was no sign of another passenger, unconscious or otherwise. "Did you at least find what we need?"

"No," her father said, but some of the tension eased out of his body at her touch. "Arvid and I found her car and followed the tracks to some sort of underground compound, but someone had set off enough explosives to cave the whole place in, probably just this morning. If she was in there, she's surely dead now."

"Did you find her body?" Joelle asked.

"Not yet," her father said. "We'll have to go back with more people and more equipment. It's going to be a lot of digging."

Scout bit her lip. She was very afraid she knew exactly who these men had been looking for and what they had found. Or rather, what they hadn't found.

They wanted the data disk. Ruth, the governor's daughter, had been taking it to the rebels. Scout didn't know what was on it; she only knew Ruth had risked much to get it out of her father's house but then had hesitated to follow through with her plans. She had worried that bringing it to the rebels wasn't the right call.

But then she had died, and the decision had been taken out of her hands.

Gertrude had always told her that most times a coincidence was just a coincidence, nothing more, nothing deeper. She had managed to talk Scout out of waiting around for fate to light up a path for her, but this sense that larger forces were leading her around by the nose, laughing as they manipulated her, was hard to shake.

She had waited her whole life for the rebels to come and make her one of them. She had been certain that was why she had lived when the rest of her family had died. She had thought her father had saved her for just that purpose.

But he hadn't. He had had no way of knowing that asteroid was on its way the morning he had given her a package to deliver to the next town and sent her and Shadow on their first solo delivery. Like Gertrude had said, he and her mother just wanted her to have a day away from her colicky little brother, and for them to have a day to give her brother their full attention. Nothing more than that.

And now, the minute the coronal mass ejection event had ended, these rebels had headed out to find information that Scout had inadvertently brought right to them by quite a different route.

Why had Tucker been there, at McFarlane's hut, at the exact time Scout had shown up there?

Scout squeezed her eyes shut tight and forced herself to stay calm. They had no reason to know she carried just what they were seeking, no reason to even suspect her. And in the morning she would be gone. She had nothing to worry about.

"Malcolm," Arvid called.

Scout opened her eyes just as Joelle's father turned to see what the other man was looking at, down on the ground. Arvid pointed at the tracks visible in the loose dust that always danced over the surface of the baked mud.

The rover tracks.

Malcolm came over to get a closer look, then the two men looked up at the rover towering over them. Scout flinched back. She was sitting in the dark with the window opened only a tiny crack—there was no way they could see her—but still she kept her head down.

"What is it?" Joelle asked, stepping closer herself. She also looked from the tracks up to the rover, but then she turned to look at her father with a questioning arch to her eyebrow.

"These look just like the tracks we followed from the wrecked town car to the demolished compound," her father said.

"That's crazy," Joelle said. "Scout's just a kid. Barely my age."

"That doesn't rule out anything, as you well know," Malcolm said. "How many bandit vehicles have you run off the road? How many trains have you left smoldering on the tracks after we made off with the cargo?"

"I never acted alone," Joelle said. "Besides, if you met her, you'd know she's not the type."

Scout smirked. It was true; she had not wrecked the town car. But she had set the explosives to bring the compound crashing down. She hadn't had the time to dig nine graves. That had been the only reason for burying the entire compound, but Malcolm and Arvid seemed to suspect some more nefarious motive.

But what was this about Joelle destroying trains? That didn't sound like the "steal from the bandits" narrative they had been selling before.

"You like her?" Malcolm asked his daughter.

Joelle's body remained as rigid as ever, her face revealing nothing. "I just met her," she said stiffly.

"Yes, but what's your read on her?" he persisted.

"Just what I said. Harmless."

"Recruiting material?"

"No." It was a very firm no.

The corner of Malcolm's mouth went up ever so slightly. "Would Tucker agree with that assessment?"

"You'd have to ask Tucker," Joelle said coolly. "But in this case, I would question his impartiality."

"Where did you say he met her?" Malcolm asked, the grin gone.

"At McFarlane's. Apparently she was looking for him too—McFarlane, I mean—but by the time she got there he was already dead."

"What did she want with McFarlane?" he asked, a dark, suspicious edge back to his voice.

Joelle shrugged. Malcolm leaned down to grasp both of her shoulders firmly. She flinched, but her father didn't seem to notice as he leaned in to speak closer to her face.

"We need to know that," he said. "We need to know what she knows, what she did, and why."

"Tucker knows more than I do," Joelle said, not dropping her eyes from her father's intense gaze.

"Well, like you said. He might not be impartial with this new girl…"

"Scout," Joelle filled in.

"Is she pretty?"

Joelle shrugged. "Not the sort of thing I would notice. Ask—"

"I will ask Tucker, about everything," Malcolm said. "Don't worry about that. And I'm sure Tucker has already wormed a goodly amount of information out of her without even knowing she might have what we're looking for. He's a sponge for intel, that boy. Very useful. I'm going to wake him up right now to find out. But I want more than one account from her, see how things compare, if she's a truth-teller."

"I think she is," Joelle said.

Malcolm looked at her closely, then released her shoulders to straighten back up. "You're a good judge of character. I've long relied on that. I'm relying on that again now. No need to wake her now. I don't want her panicking or thinking something is going on here. Just, when she's up in the morning, be there. Talk with her. Be friendly. But sound her out, see what she knows. You know what I'm looking for?"

"Of course," Joelle said. "I'll find out."

"Without her suspecting you're pumping her for information?"

"I took that as said," Joelle said.

"Of course you did. You're your mother's daughter, for sure." He gave her a fond smile, then took the bag Arvid held out for him, and the two men headed to the compound interior.

The bags over their shoulders were clinking, a dull metallic clink, as they walked. Weapons, Scout guessed.

They had gone out to meet Ruth, the governor's daughter, just as they had arranged to do before the solar storm started. Ruth had been expecting an exchange of information, a meeting around a table with pastries and coffee or tea, all parties neatly dressed and well spoken. Not that Scout had ever spoken with Ruth about it—Ruth who had been the first of all of them to die during the storm—but Scout had seen at once that Ruth was mid swan dive, about to plunge into deeper, murkier waters than she had known existed.

Scout could sympathize with that. Her life before her family had died had done nothing to prepare her for her life after.

These scarred, sun-ravaged fellows had been about to meet her, with a bag of guns apiece. The little girl Ruth had been traveling with, Clementine, had been a deadly force with or without weapons, but she had never actually been on Ruth's side. She had been an assassin who only looked like a normal tween girl, waiting for the perfect moment before she made her move.

Scout watched Joelle standing alone in the semidarkness of the canyon nook behind the rover. The sun would be up soon, and Joelle didn't look like she'd slept a wink. She had her hands in her vest pockets, her eyes on the toe of her boot gently erasing the lines from the rover treads in the dust. Then she looked up at the rover itself and Scout felt like their eyes met, just for a moment.

But maybe not. Joelle turned and walked back to the equipment room, and Scout was once more alone with her sleeping dogs.

Scout considered the massive wheel locking the gate doors together. It didn't look like anything could blast that open, even if she had kept some of Ottilie's explosives, which she hadn't. The hinges on either side that fastened the doors to the rock walls of the canyon itself were harder to judge. The bolts didn't look so very large, but there was no way to tell how deeply into the rock they penetrated. A short bolt of that width might pull free of the rock at the first push from the rover's armored body, but a longer bolt? Maybe not.

And firing up the engines, ramming the back end of the rover into the gate, gunning up the engine to batter those doors down? None of that was going to be anything like quiet.

Scout slipped down from the top bunk and went to the kitchenette to fire up the coffeemaker. She briefly regretted not bringing the last of the jolo with her before destroying the compound, but after four days of drinking bottle after bottle, she had grown sick of it. Now, not even a full day later, she was craving that double hit of sugar and caffeine again.

She would just have to make do with coffee, bitter as it was. It didn't really matter, so long as it kept her awake and alert.

While the coffee was brewing, Scout got dressed. Then she touched the disks still hidden in her pocket. They weren't compatible with anything in the rover or with Gertrude's equipment. She had no way of reading what they contained. But something in the equipment room she was never allowed to look at might be compatible.

If threatened, would she give the disks up? Without knowing what they contained, what the rebellion planned to do with the contents, how many lives might be threatened if she surrendered what she had? How could she weigh the risks?

Scout poured herself a large mug of coffee and took it to the dining nook. She took a long drink of hot, bitter coffee and sighed. She couldn't. So she had to assume the worst. She had to be prepared to do *anything* to keep every secret that had been entrusted to her.

She hoped when Liam arrived, he would have something that could read these things. And that when she finally saw what she had been carrying this entire time, she didn't have cause to regret anything she did now in ignorance. But somehow she doubted she'd be that lucky.

There was just no way she wasn't going to mess something up.

Pushing away that thought, Scout took another slug of coffee and settled in to wait for dawn and Joelle.

13

SCOUT WOKE from a nap she hadn't realized she had been taking to a soft, tinkling, chiming sound. She sat up too quickly, nearly doubled over from the sudden stab of pain in her chest from the movement, and knocked the thankfully empty coffee mug to the rover floor, where it clattered loudly.

The chiming continued with no particular pattern. Scout got to her feet and saw the dogs both sitting up on the bunk, heads tipped as they too puzzled over what they were hearing. Scout retrieved the mug from the floor and set it on the counter in the kitchenette near the sink.

Two thoughts struck her in the same moment. The first: Was the rover moving? The second: The chiming sound was the collection of sporks in the sink gently striking against each other. Scout put a hand in the sink and pushed them all away from each other until they quieted, then turned to look toward the cockpit.

It did feel like they were moving, albeit over very smooth ground. She couldn't hear the engines, but there was a gentle rocking back and forth of the rover under her feet.

Scout ran to the top of the cockpit steps to look out the panoramic window. She was still in the rebels' hideaway, parked next to the two armored jeeps.

Then the dogs started barking, suddenly and with great urgency. Scout went back down the stairs and heard a soft tapping at the rover door. She touched a hand to her pants pocket, felt the data disks still snuggled down in the depths, quite hidden, then punched the control to open the door.

Joelle looked up at her almost sheepishly. Her tactical vest was gone, replaced by a ridiculously soft-looking cardigan of a brilliant ruby red that actually looked quite nice on her. More than nice—it muted the effects of her cargo pants and combat boots and made her look thoroughly feminine, and younger.

That, and the basket in her arms, discreetly covered by a clean white tea towel. She was a fairy-tale character on her way to Grandma's house.

"I'm sorry, I didn't think I'd wake you," Joelle said, timing her words to the gaps in the barking.

"Hush, dogs," Scout said, rubbing a hand over her still-crusty hair. She was sure she looked terrible; she really needed a wash. "No worries. I was awake."

"I brought you some breakfast before you leave," Joelle said, holding up the basket. "Can I come in?"

"I suppose," Scout said, extending a hand to help Joelle step inside. The moment she was in view, both dogs jumped down from the bunk to paw at her. She tried to pet their squirming forms and remembered both of their names, but it was clear she didn't share her brother's excessive love of dogs.

"Okay, down, you two," Scout said, grabbing collars to drag dogs back from jumping all over their guest.

Joelle gave a smile of thanks. She set her basket on the middle of the dining table and pulled back the tea towel. "Do you drink coffee?" she asked with a friendly smile.

"On occasion," Scout said. "Say, did you feel the ground shaking just a moment ago?"

"Ground shaking?" Joelle repeated. The smile never left her lips, but her eyes found reasons not to meet Scout's. "No, I don't think so."

"It was shaking the whole rover. Not as bad as—" She stopped herself from saying "as yesterday," although she couldn't say why she refrained.

At any rate, Joelle didn't seem to be really listening anyway as she poured out two tiny cups of coffee from a cylindrical decanter that had been wrapped in more tea towels to keep it warm. She looked up at Scout standing uncertainly near the door and invited her to sit with a gesture.

"If it's dawn, we should be probably be going," Scout said.

"There's time yet. Let the dogs run a bit before you coop them back up in here and have some coffee with me. I brought chocolate croissants," Joelle said, the last bit in a singsong voice. She held up a crescent-shaped, dark brown pastry, wiggling it back and forth.

It smelled incredible. Scout relented, shooing the dogs outside and sliding into the seat across from Joelle. She picked up the tiny cup in front of her and looked at it dubiously.

"It's called a demitasse," Joelle told her. "It's small because the coffee I put in it is quite intense. Try it." Scout took a little sip. The caffeine rushed through her, instantly making her heart race. Joelle smiled. "These are my mom's things, the cups and the French press. She had been very particular about her coffee. She died before I was old enough to appreciate it myself, but I remember her making it when I was little. I always watched her. I think I've remembered all her little tricks correctly. It's good, right?"

"Yes," Scout said, taking another sip. "Very strong."

"The chocolate croissant recipe is hers as well. Things out here weren't so militaristic when she was still with us," Joelle said almost wistfully.

"That was before the Space Farers dropped rocks on us," Scout said.

"Yes, it was," Joelle agreed, looking down at her coffee. Scout's hands under the table clenched into fists. The desire to reach a hand across, to lend comfort, was strong. But she knew Joelle had been sent here specifically to win her over. And she was nearly succeeding, even though Scout *knew* what she was doing. Scout clenched her fists tighter, driving her nails into the flesh of her palms.

Just a little bit longer. Then she'd be free.

Joelle came out of her reverie and looked around the rover, taking in the overflowing crates of electronic parts stashed everywhere. "This isn't what I expected it to look like in here," she said.

"It's just a rover, nothing special," Scout said, then reached for another sip of coffee. The coffee had strings attached, but the rush of caffeine was worth the price.

"No, I mean, it doesn't look like you. I would think your home would be a bit more… ordered."

"Well, it's not really my home. It's only mine temporarily," she said, then immediately regretted it. She was giving Joelle information. She shouldn't be doing that. Granted, it was information Tucker already knew, but still. She had to be more careful.

She tore the croissant in front of her in half and stuffed one of the halves in her mouth. That should keep her quiet for a minute.

The croissant was still warm from the oven. She looked at the end of the half still in her hand. All those flaky layers wrapped around a dark ooze of chocolate: this wasn't the sort of thing one made in a hurry. Joelle likely hadn't slept a wink since talking with her father.

"This could be really cool if you did it up nice," Joelle said, still looking around the rover. "Put some curtains over the bunks for privacy. Paint the walls a softer color. Some pillows on these benches—"

"Like I said, this is only temporary for me," Scout said. She hoped that was still true. "The only stuff here that is really mine is in those saddlebags." She pointed over her shoulder to the floor near the bunks where she had left the twin bags from her bike. The bike was in storage over the rear treads of the rover, but she had brought her bags inside to have access to her own things.

Joelle looked like she was casting about for the next chipper thing to say, but Scout didn't want to hear it. "I'm guessing this isn't a social visit." Scout felt a stab of guilt at the sudden look of hurt in Joelle's eyes and had to bite down on her tongue to keep from apologizing. "I'm guessing you're trying to determine if I'm a security risk before you let me go. I'm sorry if I sound angry, but I was coerced into coming here in the first place and promised that I would be allowed to leave again when I wanted. Being lied to tends to make me angry."

"Tucker stretched the truth," Joelle said.

"Yes, but not just Tucker, am I right?" Scout persisted. "You guys are a team, and he's not *that* big of a loose cannon, is he?"

Joelle was shredding the croissant in her fingers, letting it crumble to pieces on the little plate edged with silver. Probably also her mother's. Scout reminded herself to stay angry.

"You're not being entirely honest either," Joelle said, dusting the last of the crumbs from her hands and giving Scout one of her more usual stern looks. Scout instantly felt more comfortable. Joelle was back to being herself.

"About what?" Scout asked.

"You know more than you're saying," Joelle said.

"About what?" Scout asked again. "I know nothing about you people or your organization, and I've tried very hard not to notice things since I got here."

"But you *do* know things," Joelle persisted. "Ken, motormouth that he is, blabbed about the girl assassins the Space Farers have been sending into prominent Planet Dweller residences. Nearly no one on the surface knows about that. Barely any Space Farers know about that, only the ones in certain upper circles of their command structure. And yet you knew about that."

"I've heard rumors," Scout said vaguely.

"No, you know more than that," Joelle said, nearly making Scout squirm under the intensity of her gaze. "When Ken said that one of those agents had infiltrated the governor's home, you said 'not anymore.' What did you mean by that? Because, to my ears, that sounds like you have some pretty specific knowledge. And if you were telling the truth, you know more than we do."

"I don't remember saying that," Scout said honestly.

"You did. At dinner, you said just that."

Scout ducked her head to block out those intense eyes and played back her memories from the night before. Oh. Yes, she had said that. Joelle gave a triumphant smile as Scout failed to keep her face neutral at the memory.

"I do deliveries between cities and towns all over this part of the planet," Scout said. "I hear lots of things in lots of places. Honestly, I don't remember where I hear everything. There are rumors everywhere."

"I don't believe you heard such an incredibly specific, timely, and correct rumor," Joelle said.

"How do you know it's correct?" Scout countered. Joelle frowned. Scout bit her lip to prevent her own triumphant smile from emerging. She didn't know, not for sure. At least, not that the girl assassins were dead now.

"What happened to you during the storm?" Joelle asked. Scout couldn't read her tone. Her eyes were as hard as ever, but there was empathy in her voice, like she knew it had been bad and was truly trying to help. Scout bit her lip even harder.

"I'm not talking about that," Scout said. "I won't."

"You talked about it to Tucker," Joelle said.

"Not really."

"You did," Joelle said. Then, to Scout's surprise, she heaved a sigh. "Listen—"

"Knock, knock," Tucker said from the open doorway. "Are you two having a breakfast party without me?"

"Not really a party, no," Scout said. "But there's food if you want some."

"I don't want to interrupt," Tucker said, holding up his hands as if in surrender. He gave Scout a grin she had no desire to return, then looked to Joelle. Joelle was slumped back in her seat, arms crossed as she stared at the remains of her croissant. "Joelle? Malcolm was looking for you. I think he needs a thing or something?"

"Is that so," Joelle said, her voice completely flat. But she got to her feet, brushing past Tucker as she jumped down and he climbed into the rover. She turned to shoot him an inscrutable look before wrapping the cardigan more snugly around her and disappearing from view.

Tucker turned to Scout with a shrug. "She gets moods. Especially when she breaks out her mother's stuff. Although I do like that color on her. Can I sit?"

Scout waved a hand he took for an affirmative and he sat across from her. He looked into the empty demitasse Joelle had left behind and wiped the rim clean with the end of his shirt before filling it from the decanter.

"Was she giving you the first degree?" he asked as he peeked inside the basket and fetched one of the remaining croissants.

"I guess. But why?"

Tucker, mouth full of pastry, just shrugged. "She likes to be very sure," he said around chewing.

"You promised me I could go," she reminded him.

"I know. That's still going to happen," he said, but she just scoffed and tried not to let him see how hard she blinked her eyes. "It is." He reached across the table to catch one of her hands and give it a squeeze.

She let him, but she kind of hated herself for it. This wasn't the time to start getting feelings or attachments. Especially not with this guy who may or may not be lying to her.

"I just want to go," she said.

"I know," he said.

"Not just from here, from this entire world," Scout said. "I'm done with being here. I haven't had a place here since my family died. I've just been waiting. And I'm so sick of waiting."

Some strange emotion rippled over Tucker's face but was gone too quickly for Scout to identify it. It was like he tucked it away before pushing forward again with his benign charm.

"I made a promise," he said. He was probably going to say more, but Scout didn't want to hear it. No more empty reassurances. She pulled her hand out of his very nicely warm grasp and tucked it back under the table with the other.

"Why were you at McFarlane's hut yesterday?" she asked.

"Hmm?" he responded, but he had stuffed another bite of croissant into his mouth with suspicious haste.

"There was a reason. You must have left here the moment the storm passed to get there in time. Why the hurry?"

"He owed us something," he said vaguely. "I was going to fetch it."

"For Malcolm?" He blinked, his face perhaps too carefully blank, and she let it go. "There was nothing of any value in his hut," she pointed out instead.

"Yes, I noticed that," Tucker said with nicely contained sarcasm. "Not only did he stiff us, he was never going to deliver in the first place. I'm not sorry he's dead."

"I am," Scout said. "He had crimes to be held accountable for."

"More than you know," Tucker said.

"More than *you* know," Scout countered angrily. "A galactic marshal was here specifically to find him and bring him back to justice. He destroyed the lives of people all over the galaxy, not just this miserable heat sink of a planet."

"I'm sorry. I'm not trying to be glib," Tucker said. "I knew he wasn't from around here. I used to like to be the one Malcolm sent to negotiate deals with him. If McFarlane wasn't drinking and was in a reasonably good mood, I could get him to tell me stories of other worlds. Hell, maybe he made them all up, I don't know, but I loved those stories. I'd love to see for myself which ones are true."

Scout swallowed once or twice and got her emotions back under control. "Tucker, what did you negotiate with him for?"

"I'm sorry. If it were just me, I'd tell you, but I can't tell other people's secrets. Especially if it might put them in danger. I just can't."

Scout nodded. He sounded sincere, but then he always sounded sincere.

"You look like you have one more question," he said mildly.

Scout swallowed. There was really only one question that mattered. "Will you swear to me that you had nothing to do with McFarlane being dead?"

Tucker had a mouthful of croissant, so it took a moment for him to answer. When he did, he leaned forward to grasp her hand again and hit her with the full intensity of those gray eyes.

"Scout Shannon, I solemnly swear to you, I never set foot inside Farlane McFarlane's hut until the moment I found you there."

"So you didn't kill him?"

"Considering I'm the one who found you with a gun in your hand standing over his dead body, and you keep telling me all the bad things he's done all over the galaxy, I find it odd I'm not the one peppering you with questions and accusations. I guess it's because I trust you."

Scout scowled. "I didn't draw the gun until you startled me."

"If you say so." Tucker shrugged and reached for the last croissant.

"I should go find my dogs," she said, getting up from the table.

"The last I saw, they were patrolling the storage warehouse with Reggie. I'll show you."

Scout hopped out of the rover and turned to wait as Tucker chugged down the last of his coffee and jumped down after her. He brushed back the lock of dark hair that had fallen over his forehead, then thrust his hands into his pockets. It was barely dawn, and the air was still cold. Then he nudged Scout's arm with his elbow to indicate that she should follow him.

"Do you truly want to leave this place?" Scout asked as she fell in step beside him.

"Malcolm and the others have been like a family to me," Tucker said, and Scout nodded. The stomach-clenching feeling of disappointment surprised her. Had she really thought he'd leave with her? After just a day? "But they're not my family, not really," Tucker went on. "I would do anything to keep them safe, but I don't think I'll ever really feel like I belong here. Do you know what I mean?"

"Yes," Scout said. "I think I do."

She had put her freezing hands into her own pockets, fingertips brushing the data disks. That was what she had to keep safe. But it wasn't really connecting her to anything, not in a belonging sort of way. No one had entrusted these things to her. They had just sort of fallen into her lap.

She took her hands back out of her pockets and caught the sleeve of Tucker's shirt, bringing them both to a halt. He turned to look at her and Scout stumbled over her words in the sudden realization of how close they were standing to each other. She wanted to take half a step back. It would certainly be easier to talk to him if she did; he was a full head taller than she was.

But she also didn't want to step away.

"Listen," she said, and he leaned in closer, his eyes intent on hers.

Then the canyon around them began to echo with the grinding metallic groan of the gate unlatching and swinging open. Scout thought at first that it was Joelle, finally releasing her, if a moment or two sooner than Scout would have liked.

Then Scout realized what she had failed to notice earlier when she had looked out the rover window to determine if she was moving or not. The motorcycles hadn't been in their place between the rover and the two jeeps.

Someone had gotten them outside in the early morning hours without making a sound, when Scout had been certain she wasn't even sleeping. And now they were back, the two of them on either side of some sort of yoke, towing a wheeled platform.

And on the platform was a town car. It was covered in red dust after spending several days out in the elements, but it was recognizably luxurious under that coating. Few owned such fine vehicles. Really, only the governor of the colonies of Amatheon, perhaps one or two of the mayors of the larger cities.

But Scout didn't have to speculate about the ownership or even wonder how such a rare vehicle had ended up so far from where the upper class lived and played. She recognized the town car straight away, although she had only seen it once before. It had belonged to Ruth, the governor's daughter. She had gotten stranded in it just before the storm.

She had been driving it out to the hills to meet with the rebels. These rebels.

14

THE ROAR of engines made speech impossible until Ken and Bente had unyoked their bikes and parked them on the other side of the rover. Tucker tugged Scout's sleeve, wanting her to follow him as he went to take a closer look at the town car. Scout dug her hands deep into her pockets but stayed where she was near the door to the equipment room. Then someone jostled her. The sound of their approaching footsteps had been drowned out by the still-droning engines, and Scout quickly stumbled out of the way.

If Malcolm noticed that he had bowled her over coming out of the equipment room, he didn't react or even look back to see what he had collided with. Scout stepped back out of the doorway in case others would be following in his wake, slumping against the wall and trying not to be noticed.

Then the two bikes shut off, one after the other. The drone of the morning insects could just be heard in the distance. There was no grass growing in the little nook behind the gate, so they had no home here.

"Perfect," Malcolm said, clapping his hands as he approached the dusty town car. Ken and Bente emerged from behind the rover, goggles dangling around their necks as they threw back the hoods of their dusters and pulled off their cap-like helmets.

"It was just where you said it was," Ken said. "Jacked up on a rock, but Bente got it moved all right. We searched the area in case anything had been dropped nearby, but there wasn't anything."

"No, I didn't expect that there would be," Malcolm said. "There were only two or three footprints between the town car and the rover tracks. She was definitely picked up and transported."

"Rescued or kidnapped?" Ken wondered. "If she had been chased and run off the road onto the rock—"

"There would have been more tracks in the road," Malcolm cut him off. "It's not a road that sees a lot of traffic. But there were just the town car tracks and then the rover."

"So it was a rescue. But did she know her rescuers or not?" Ken said.

"That's exactly the question," Malcolm said. "If they were friends, she would probably have taken what she had with her. She would feel safe. But if they were strangers, if she thought they might be a threat, she might have hidden what she had in the town car so it wouldn't fall into their hands. That's why you are going to strip this thing down to the bones. We need to be sure."

"These newer models have a much more complex design than the older ones," Ken said. "More places to stash things. It could take all day."

"Luckily, you have nowhere else to go," Malcolm said, clapping him on the shoulder.

A flicker of motion caught the corner of Scout's eye and she turned her head to see Arvid tossing canvas bags out the door, making a rough sort of pile outside the equipment room. The bags fell heavily, the pieces inside clanging against each other. Maybe weapons, maybe something else. Definitely not the same bags they had carried inside the night before.

"Tucker, give Arvid a hand with those," Malcolm said.

Tucker had opened the town car door and was running his hands over the panels on the inside, but quickly jumped at Malcolm's command. "Give us a hand?" he said to Scout as he threw a bag over each shoulder.

She really wished she could remain unseen in the corner, but not complying with such a benign request was likely to draw even more attention. She bent and wrapped her arms around one of the sacks, then staggered after Tucker toward the jeep parked nearest the gate.

"What's in here?" she whispered to Tucker as she put her bag next to his two in the back of the jeep. Tucker shrugged, uninterested.

Arvid came up behind them and Scout stepped aside so he could drop the last two bags into the jeep. He took a moment to adjust the bags more securely, then stepped back and seemed to finally see Scout standing there.

"Hi," Scout said uncertainly. He had spoken the night before, so he wasn't as laconic as his niece, but the eyes assessing her were not exactly friendly either.

"This is Scout," Tucker said. "You've already met her dogs."

Arvid nodded but continued looking Scout over. Scout thrust her hands back into her pockets. The fingers of one hand brushed against the data disks, the other the lens that was required to operate any of the equipment on Gertrude's belt.

The belt—she had left it hanging from its hook when she had followed Tucker out of the rover.

Perhaps it was better she wasn't wearing it now. The two grown-ups hadn't seen all of her off-world gadgets yet. Had the others told them about what she had? No one had asked her about any of it, not even Tucker, and yet she doubted very much they hadn't noticed any of it.

"Scout," Malcolm said, his deep voice echoing through the canyon nook. "The kids have been telling me all about you."

Scout swallowed hard. There was no way she could safely respond to that without knowing what exactly they had said. Then Malcolm walked over to stand towering over her.

He was a commanding figure, tall and the sort of thin that's all wiry muscle, with a booming voice and an air of expecting to be obeyed. She reversed her assessment from the night before: He was like Joelle but bigger. But there was nothing particularly aggressive about his demeanor as he walked up to her. He seemed just to want to formally greet her, a visitor to his home.

So Scout was a little startled when Tucker took a step to position himself half in front of her, drawing himself up taller. Not that it helped much; Malcolm was twice his size. Malcolm stopped in front of Tucker, amusement dancing in his eyes. Then he put out a hand and gently pushed Tucker to one side so he had an unobstructed view of Scout.

Scout endured her second thorough inspection in as many minutes. He even reached out and knocked her hat back, just as Tucker had done the day before.

"Not what I was expecting," he said in the end and turned his back on her. Scout felt her cheeks flushing as she put her hat back on her head. What did that mean?

"Sir, I thank you for your hospitality, but I really need to be moving on. I have a place to be."

Malcolm turned back to look at her again. Scout stiffened her spine and refused to drop her eyes.

"No. Not now," he said.

"Sir—"

"Not until we have in hand what we need to have in hand," he said.

"I don't even know what that means," Scout said, hoping she sounded more clueless than she felt.

"You want to get out of here?" he asked. Scout nodded. "You want to get out of here in a hurry?" Scout nodded again. "Then help the others tear this car down. No one is leaving here until I have what I need."

"Sir—" she started again, but this time when he turned back to her, his eyes were so furious she did fall silent.

"Malcolm, I did promise her," Tucker said, gently, reasonably.

Malcolm turned that fiery gaze onto Tucker, who flinched ever so slightly but didn't back down.

"Don't go making promises you can't keep," Malcolm said, raising a warning finger. "You've already let me down once today."

"That wasn't my fault—"

But Malcolm wasn't hearing it. "Find what I need. Until I have it, all of these doors are staying locked." As if to prove his point, he took a small controller out of his pocket and pushed a button.

So far as Scout could see, nothing happened. But the slump to Tucker's shoulders spoke differently.

Malcolm turned to march back over to where Bente and Ken were huddled over the toolbox, Bente listening intently to whatever Ken was whispering to her as he dug through the tools. Scout turned to stand in front of Tucker, close enough that he couldn't avoid looking back at her. He shook his head sadly, and she fought the sudden urge to kick him in the shins.

"You two have this in hand?" Malcolm was booming at Ken and Bente. Arvid brushed past Scout to climb up into the passenger seat of the jeep.

"We've got it," Joelle said as she emerged from the equipment room. The red sweater was gone, the tactical vest back in its place. "Do you need one of us to go with you?"

"No, we've got help meeting us on the way," her father said. "I expect to see this car broken down into the smallest possible pieces by the time I get back. If you should find anything, Joelle, send me a signal."

"Wilco," Joelle said.

Malcolm was about to step inside the jeep, but stopped to look back at them all. Ken and Bente stopped consulting on tools to give him their attention. Reggie even appeared in the doorway behind his sister, Gert and Shadow peering around his ankles.

"I don't think I need to impress the importance of all this on you. We all know where things are heading." They all nodded their heads, but he went on anyway, his voice echoing through the canyon. "War."

Scout was still standing with her nose centimeters from Tucker's chin, watching his face. He had crossed his arms and closed his eyes as Malcolm started speaking, but he did not flinch at the word "war."

"The governor's daughter was coming to meet us, as arranged, but she never arrived. And I'm fairly certain she was not alone in this car. One of those murderous girls was with her. She was not the intended target, but with the governor behind locked doors, the target might change. And that would be very bad for our cause."

Tucker had turned to look at Malcolm but was keeping his face carefully impassive. Scout looked to see what the others were doing. Ken and Bente had stopped with tools in hand to listen, their faces also carefully blank.

Joelle turned to shoo her brother away from the doorway behind her, but when she turned back, she didn't meet her father's eyes. She kept her gaze fixed on a point on the ground just in front of him, arms crossed. Scout couldn't say for sure, but she seemed to be biting her lip.

"But we don't know if she's dead," Malcolm went on, his eyes moving from one of them to the next as he spoke. "Or what happened to what she intended to bring us. That is the most important thing now. War is inevitable. We are too few to change that fate. But hidden as we are, we are safe. We must make the others safe, too. What happened before cannot be allowed to happen again. Whatever the cost. No sacrifice is too great to see that work done."

His voice was booming now, his hands in fists, his eyes on the sky as he spoke.

"And those who have to die to keep our people safe, they will die. Guilty or innocent, for the sake of our people, they will die."

Scout saw something flicker over Joelle's face, and her eyes went to Scout's. The harsh sternness was still there, but there was a crinkling at the corners that almost looked like concern. Malcolm had fallen silent, but the words he was leaving yet to be spoken seemed to hover like a massive hammer about to drop and crush them all.

Scout turned away from Joelle's eyes to see that Malcolm had been staring at her for some time, waiting for her to turn and see.

Was she the one who would have to die? Why?

But Malcolm, sudden storm of fervent emotion apparently gone, just turned his attention back to Ken and Bente. "Get going on that car."

Ken saluted with the wrench in his hand, and Bente nodded. Then Malcolm dropped into the jeep's driver's seat and fired up the engine. The wheels spun, filling the air with red dust. Then they were gone, and the gate was closing.

"Wait!" Scout shouted, throwing up her arms as if she could stop those massive metal doors from closing.

"They can't be stopped," Joelle said. "I'm sorry."

Scout whistled for her dogs and ran for the rapidly diminishing gap between the doors. To hell with the rover. She had the coordinates in the tablet on her belt and could walk day and night if she had to.

Scout took two steps and then stopped. The coordinates were on the tablet, and the tablet was on the belt, but the belt was in the rover. She would never reach it in time.

The gate shut with that deafening clang followed by the grinding of the lock engaging.

Scout spun to glare at Joelle.

"It's not up to me," Joelle said, her tone and her face both cold and steely. "My father has all the controls. There's nothing I can do." She was bracing herself as if waiting for Scout to take a swing at her, and only then did Scout realize her hands were balled into fists. She took a breath and forced her fingers to splay wide at her hips.

"You're not going to find anything in that car," Scout said.

"You know this for a fact?" Joelle asked. "Because if you do, you can save us all a lot of time. You can save us a lot of everything if you'd just tell us what you know."

"Nothing I know is going to help you," Scout said. "Seriously, what was that speech?"

"He's been under stress," Ken said, but he flinched when both Joelle and Tucker turned to glare at him.

"Is that a secret, too?" Scout asked.

"It's not just stress," Joelle said, turning her glare onto Tucker.

"I only did what he asked me to," Tucker said. "He makes the decisions that are best for him."

"Not for a minute do I believe you think what you've been bringing him is 'the best for him,'" Joelle said.

"He makes the decisions—" Tucker started to say again, but Joelle cut him off with one upward motion of her hand.

"You told me before there was another way out of here?" Scout said after a painfully long moment of no one else saying a word.

"They're all locked now," Tucker said.

"Show me," Scout said.

Tucker looked to Joelle. Joelle first shrugged, then nodded, then turned to head back into the equipment room.

"There's the gate," Tucker said, pointing at it as he continued walking away from it, along the outer wall of the compound. Scout followed, her dogs close at her heels. There was a small building tucked into the corner, like a watchman's station. Tucker stepped inside, but it was too small for Scout to get more than half of her body in after him. "The gate controls are here, but like Joelle told you, Malcolm locked them down." He pressed a few buttons that protested with red lights and negative beeping noises.

Then he turned to half sit on the control panel and pointed at the back wall. "There's a crawl space that leads to a hidden doorway in the canyon." Scout could just make out the outline. Tucker bent to push at it, but it remained locked.

"There are others," Scout said with certainty.

Tucker nodded grimly, then waited for her to step aside so he could lead the way back through the equipment room, past the closed offices and the one open one where Joelle was standing behind Reggie sitting at the desk and tapping at a computer terminal. Then they continued on through the kitchen to the room where the dogs had gone hunting the night before.

There was a row of refrigerators and freezers near the door, but further in it was more like a warehouse, crates and boxes stacked on pallets to keep them up off the earthen floor. Scout could hear scuttling and both of the dogs raced past her and Tucker to chase something further in the dark depths of the room.

"Big space," Scout said.

"Those stairs lead up to the barracks. And this is the last door out," Tucker said, pointing to the wall to their left. Scout walked over to it. The stairway was steep, with handrails on either side, hugging close to the wall. Further along the wall at the very edge of the room was a hatch, a heavy door with a wheel in the center. The wheel wouldn't turn in either direction, but then the red light centered over the doorway was probably meant to tell her that.

She turned to glare at Tucker again. She had to. If she let that anger go, she was going to start feeling the despair.

"Why did you do this?" she asked, hoping he didn't hear how her voice was about to crack.

"Come on," he said, tugging at her sleeve again. "Your dogs will be okay in here. I want to show you something."

He crossed the warehouse, heading for the far wall. It went further than Scout was expecting, and she guessed they were now inside the canyon wall that formed the back of the nook where the vehicles were parked. The walls were less squared off here, the ceiling coming down in irregular lumps and crags more like a natural cavern. Tucker led her around a larger outcropping of yellow rock and then up a steep slope that looked like it had been carved out by a stream once upon a time.

She saw sunlight up ahead. Then they were up in it, high atop the canyon. The sun was blinding, but even without a hat, Tucker seemed less bothered by it than she. He took her hand to guide her further, then caught her in his arms before she took a step too far.

"Look," he said.

She blinked, the sunlight bouncing off the yellow rock so bright it brought tears to her eyes. It was nearly noon. Already noon, a day half gone, and she trapped immobile, nowhere near the meeting point.

Then she blinked again and started to make out features of the world around her. The canyon nook full of vehicles was below her, spread out under her feet. She could follow the contours of the canyon with her eyes, even see the cloud of dust that hid Malcolm and Arvid in their jeep heading back to the compound Scout had tried to bury with Ottilie's explosives.

Having seen every detail of the compound and dust trail, her eyes at last settled on the canyon walls themselves. They gleamed brightly in the morning sun, so many bands of colors. How could stone come in so many colors? Not even in her dreams had she ever seen such a magical sight.

It brought a tear to her eye, but she had to shut her eyes to it. Block it out; not notice it. It was a distraction when what she needed was an escape.

Scout pushed away Tucker's hands on her shoulders and walked along the edge of the ridge. It was a sheer drop down to the compound below, then a sheer drop down to the canyon she had entered from.

And the back side was even worse. There was a chasm so deep the bottom was lost to shadows.

Scout walked the entire way around, but there was no path to level ground, no way out of this complex but through the locked doors. She ended up back where she started, where Tucker waited for her.

"I'm sorry," he said.

"Not as sorry as I am." Scout turned her back on him and went back down the tunnel to find her dogs.

                                    15

SCOUT'S FEET threatened to slip out from under her as she tried to make her way back down the slope into the cavernous part of the warehouse. The floor of the tunnel was a steep groove, sloping up to the walls on both sides but not evenly, and the bottom was filled with dust, sand, and fine gravel too small to see. It was definitely there, though, moving around under the soles of her boots. Scout put a hand on each wall as she carefully made her way down.

After the heat of the noonday sun, the cool of the cavern was quite pleasant, but that heat was going to drive Tucker inside after her soon enough, so she kept moving, past the natural rock formations to where the walls were squared off. She took the first turn through rows of shelving, then another and another until she was certain Tucker would not find her should he try to follow her.

She was done talking with him.

She found a crate left sitting on the floor in one dark corner and sat down on it, drawing her knees up to her chest and resting her chin on them while she tried to think things through. The air was cool but had a musty smell, a bit like a small rodent had died and was slowly decomposing somewhere just out of sight, but also like something organic inside one of the containers had gone mildewy. She didn't investigate; if it smelled this bad while locked away, she had no interest in getting a lungful when she took off the lid of whatever box it was hiding in.

She heard footsteps. Tucker, coming back down and into the warehouse. He didn't pause, just kept walking past the food storage to the kitchen. There was a soft murmur of voices. She couldn't make out any words, but she reckoned the other speaker was Ken. It sounded like his tone and that voice went on quite a bit longer than Tucker's softer replies.

Then that sound too faded away. Scout wrapped her arms around her legs and leaned against the heavy support of the shelving unit beside her, letting her head rest against it. She had gotten maybe an hour's worth of sleep. She needed far more.

She had only dozed off for a moment when a fury of skittering woke her. Something small was running her way, pursued by two dogs. Shadow was intent on his prey, keeping his nose low to the ground even as he ran, but Gert galloped along behind, punctuating her trot with excited barks. Not her frightening hellhound woof, but a delighted yap that was probably more terrifying for the poor rodent about to be played with to death.

"Scout!"

Scout lifted her head, then toyed with the idea of not answering Joelle's call. But what good would that do? Even if they didn't have cameras in here watching her already, it wouldn't take long to search the place. Scout got to her feet and stretched out her back, then walked back to the kitchen.

Joelle was in the doorway. Relief washed over her face when she saw Scout emerge from the shadows.

"What is it?" Scout asked.

"Tucker and Ken have gone out on a mission," Joelle said. "I wanted to see if you would like to help Bente and me with a thing. I know you're going to want to tell me to stuff it," she said as Scout opened her mouth, "but please consider it. It would help my father's judgment of you a lot if he knew you were pitching in."

Scout wanted to snap back that she scarcely cared how her probably insane father judged her, but she remembered he was the one holding all the keys.

"What sort of thing?" Scout asked. "Robbing trains?"

"No, not robbing trains," Joelle said. "No need. As you saw in our warehouse, we're well stocked on everything."

"Stripping the town car?"

"No, that's been done. Bente came up with a… faster method."

"Did they find anything?" Scout asked, trying to sound like she didn't already know the answer.

"No. Not yet."

"So this thing…?"

"What we need to do is more an act of rebellion than thievery or vandalism," Joelle said. "And we'll be doing it in the kitchen."

"How do you rebel from a kitchen?" Scout asked.

"Come on and I'll show you," Joelle said, stepping back from the doorway. Scout was curious enough to follow her.

Somewhere behind her, something squeaked and then died. That had to be Shadow's work. His headshake took them out nearly instantly. Gert, on the other hand—with her toss-up-in-the-air-and-fail-to-catch-it technique—tended to give her playthings a long, slow death.

"You really do have a rodent problem," Scout said as she followed Joelle back into the kitchen.

"It's recent," Joelle said. "And they're not getting into the food. That's all well sealed."

"Yes, Tucker said something like that," Scout said. "They didn't come here with the food you stole, he said. Something was driving them here?"

"Tucker says a lot," Joelle said with an air of dropping the subject. Apparently, her new friendliness had defined limits.

Joelle walked over to the long table where they had eaten the night before. Bente was setting out blocks of paper, using the knife from her belt to cut away the bindings that held the stacks perfectly square.

"Where's Reggie?" Scout asked.

"He's in his office. He attends a school in the city remotely," Joelle said. "The rest of us qualified for early graduation, but he's young yet and still has a ways to go."

"School," Scout said. Her own school days had ended the day the Space Farers dropped an asteroid on her city. There had never been a chance to finish her education. She felt the others watching her and was afraid her cheeks were flushed. She had no reason to be embarrassed over what she couldn't control, and yet she was. "What's all this?" she asked to draw their attention back to the table and not her face.

Bente handed her one sheet of paper. It was a bright neon pink. The Space Farer logo was emblazoned across the top, and the entire thing was done in the weird font they preferred, all curves and long horizontal lines so that lines of texts looked like high-speed trains racing across the page.

"Propaganda," Joelle said as Scout's eyes swept down the page. "The Planet Dweller government blocks all their transmissions, so the Space Farers have taken to printing things up. They like to drop these on the towns from the sky. They even get them to blow through the streets in the domed cities."

"They're threatening to knock the satellites out of orbit if we don't double the food shipments," Scout said. "Is this legit?"

"What do you think?" Joelle asked, her face carefully blank. Bente beside her imitated the expression, even blinking her blue eyes with feigned innocence.

"First of all, why would you steal their propaganda?" Scout said, examining the page. The paper had a heavy quality to it. That, the logo, the font—it all felt like the real thing. She had touched missives from space before, and if this was counterfeit, it was quite good.

"Propaganda is our greatest weapon," Joelle said. "With our numbers so few, it's nearly our only weapon. That and information."

Scout ignored that obvious attempt at getting her to tell what she knew. "So they're targeting the satellites that form the magnetic shield? If they knock those down, they can't be replaced. There's no coming back from that." Scout turned her attention from the paper in her hands back to the two girls watching her. "That's a hell of a threat. And from what I've seen, no one down here is capable of doubling the food shipments, anyway. The Space Farers would never get what they want. It's impossible."

"It's a very foolish threat," Joelle agreed.

"So it is legit?" Scout asked again.

Joelle just tipped her head to one side, not affirming or denying.

Scout looked down at the page again. "Would you fabricate this just to sow chaos?"

"If we did, it would be quite effective, don't you think?"

"Too effective," Scout said, examining the paper. "This is a really good counterfeit."

"As it so happens, it's not counterfeit," Joelle told her. "We stole it from the Space Farers. Apparently, they had toyed with the idea of unleashing this threat, but someone backed off. Not enough to destroy these, but enough for them to warehouse them for another time."

"Warehouse them on the surface?" Scout asked.

Joelle ignored the question. "They fell into our hands. Our job is to get them out to the people. We're attaching this card to each," she said, handing an index card full of writing to Scout. The back could be peeled away to expose an adhesive. Scout glanced over it, but Joelle explained it anyway. "The people should know the threat is out there. They should be prepared. We need to take steps to secure our own magnetic shield. This is a call to start that dialog. The planetary government isn't doing a thing, so we're going to the people, to get them riled up to take action themselves. That's how we rebel."

"Isn't there a more efficient way to spread the word?" Scout asked.

"Ken and some of the other tech heads have been trying to find ways to get into the electronic systems and disseminate information, but so far, they haven't had more than minimal luck with it. Plus, this way everyone gets a piece of actual Space Farer print in their hands. It's more convincing that way, don't you think?" Scout supposed that was true.

"The shield is failing already, isn't it?" she said. "The storms are harder, longer, and more frequent. Have they knocked some satellites down already?"

Joelle glanced over at Bente and Bente raised her chin, encouraging her to go on. "We don't know. Not for sure. Do you know anything about life up there?"

"Not really. The women who owned the rover, one of them was a Space Farer. But she'd been living down here since the war ended. She didn't talk about her prior life much." Ebba hadn't said much about her life in space, but the others had made lots of accusations. Scout didn't know how many of them were true. Like whether Ebba had been part of the command structure that had dropped asteroids on the cities. On Scout's family. Tucker's family. Joelle's mother, too, for that matter.

"The war never ended," Joelle said. "Will you help us? We don't want these flyers to get dispersed without the cards to explain or there might be a panic."

"There might be a panic anyway," Scout said. "Like you said, it was a legitimate threat."

"If we get these out, people will have time to react. And to *think* before they react," Joelle said. "Will you help us?"

Her voice was almost desperately earnest. Too much for such a small ask. Scout reckoned it was a long road that ended at robbing trains, but this was probably where it started.

On the other hand, people did need to know. She had tuned out political talk most of her life, but if the last few days had taught her anything, it was that politics were important and far too few people were paying attention. "Where are you going to distribute these?" she asked at last.

"Everywhere we can," Joelle said. "The people outside of the cities need to know because they depend on that magnetic shield. Their only shelter is underground, and that can never be more than temporary. Without the shield, their lives aren't possible. But the people in the cities should know too. If they are dropping more shit from space, they're going to be dropping it on the cities. Someone will be picking these up in the morning; we have to have them bundled and ready by then."

"I think you're right, this is important," Scout said and slid onto the bench across from the two of them to start attaching the little cards to the corner of the pink flyers. Joelle gave her a grateful smile and she and Bente also got to work. "So, this is the rebellion?" Scout said.

"Part of it," Joelle said. "The most important part, in my view. We have to inform people and get them to start changing their minds about things."

"But then there's also robbing trains," Scout said.

"That's not as self-serving as you'd think," Joelle said. "We acquired most of what you saw in the warehouse just before the last storm drove us into the shelter for four days. As soon as my father has this other problem locked down, we'll be distributing this to the communities that need it. We don't keep more than we need, and we don't profit from any of it."

"So why steal it at all?" Scout asked.

"The governor is getting more than his fair share. The bandits have been robbing him for a while now. We just started beating the bandits to the punch. They were selling what they took on the black market for quite a lot of cash. My father ignored it for a long time, because people stealing from the governor is not exactly counter to our mission, you know? But then the black-market money got too good, and the bandits started robbing *all* the trains. That's when we got involved."

"Very noble," Scout said.

"I can't sit by and do nothing," Joelle said, annoyed at Scout's flippant tone.

"There has to be more going on here than that, though," Scout said. "Because that all sounds reasonable and upstanding and *noble*. But then I'm being held prisoner for no reason, after being lured here, and that act is none of those things. You can see why I'm suspicious of what else might be going on."

"Tucker brought you here without approval," Joelle said.

"Hey, I love the 'blame Tucker' game as well as anyone—" Scout began, but Joelle talked over her.

"He says he intended for you to drop him off in the canyon without ever seeing where we were, but that the dogs made him nervous and he got distracted and didn't wave off Ken and Bente in time."

"Ah," Scout said, looking up at them both. That had been bothering her for some time: Tucker's on-and-off fear of her dogs. "You believe that?"

Joelle pursed her lips tightly. Bente looked over at her as if she, too, wanted to hear the answer.

"Tucker got bit by a dog when he was little," Joelle said.

"So he told me. And showed me," Scout said. "But I can't help noticing he's had no real fear of my dogs since that moment. You're going to tell me my dogs are good dogs and so therapeutic that one encounter with them cures lifelong phobias?"

"No," Joelle said.

"So Tucker lied," Scout said.

"No," Joelle said quickly. "It's complicated. You don't know Tucker, and he's hard to explain."

Bente made a sound suspiciously like a chuckle, but when Scout looked her way, she was innocently going about her work.

"It doesn't really matter now," Joelle said. "My father has strict rules. The minute you came inside that gate… no, the minute you even saw that there was a gate, we couldn't let you go."

"You acted like you could," Scout said. "You acted like you were going to. Did you make up seeing movement on your equipment?"

"No," Joelle said. "I was hoping I could sneak you out and swear the others to secrecy, and my father would never know you were ever here. It was a dumb idea; it would have never worked. He has to make that decision. He's in charge. But I promise, that's not as bad as it sounds. He just needs to talk to you one-on-one and get a feel for you. But there's a lot going on right now that he has to focus on first."

"Yes, he seems… focused," Scout said diplomatically.

"He's just upset," Joelle said, and now it was her turn to not meet Scout's eyes. "Things haven't been going our way lately. A lot of people have left the cause, as you can probably tell. This place was built to hold fifty people, but there are only seven of us and most of us are teens."

"Actually, that just makes me extra freaked out by the 'glory to all martyrs' speech he gave this morning," Scout said.

"It'll be fine," Joelle said, focused on her hands binding a stack of papers. "He just needs to find what he's looking for and then he'll talk to you about the importance of keeping our location secret and then everything will be fine."

But Bente was looking over at Joelle with deep sympathy. Scout doubted Joelle's father was anywhere near being fine.

Scout and Bente were attaching the last few cards to the remaining flyers, and Joelle was stacking the finished bundles on a handcart when Shadow and Gert came barreling into the kitchen.

"What's with them?" Joelle asked as they ran past her. Scout got up from the bench to intercept them and they slid to a halt to jump all over her.

"Something has them spooked," Scout said.

"Something in the warehouse?" Joelle said with a frown.

But Scout didn't think so. Gert's paws knocked her off-balance, and she sprawled back on the floor to find Shadow leaping into her arms, pounding his entire body against her bruised chest. Gert burrowed in close between Scout's knees, pressing in tight under Shadow's trembling body.

No mere animal would upset the two of them this much. It was like the entire world was all of a sudden freaking them out, their eyes huge. Shadow shook and shook in Scout's arms and Gert whined fearfully.

Then the entire world freaked out Scout too when it began quaking beneath her.

16

THIS TIME, Scout *knew* she was feeling the ground moving underneath her. She wasn't in a rover, moving or otherwise. There was no other explanation. The dishes inside the cupboards were rattling, and something in the warehouse fell to the ground with a thump. Bente stood with both hands planted on the tabletop like that was lending her desperately needed stability. Joelle caught the cart before it could start rolling away from her.

Then the shaking stopped as inexplicably as it had begun. Joelle stayed as she was for another moment to be sure everything was going to stay still, then went back to loading up the cart as if nothing had happened.

Scout looked over at Bente. Bente looked a bit green, like the earth shaking had just made her seasick, but when she saw Scout watching her, she swallowed hard and continued with her work.

"Come on," Scout said to them, hugging both of her nervous little dogs. "You can't tell me you didn't feel that."

"It's nothing to worry about," Joelle said.

"Happens all the time, does it?" Scout asked. "As opposed to when it happened this morning and you pretended like it didn't?"

"Joelle?" Reggie asked anxiously. He was standing in the hall, hugging the doorway of one of the offices.

"It's all done now, Reggie. You can get back to school," Joelle said. Reggie looked unconvinced, but just nodded and went back into the little room, closing the door. The smile she had given him quickly melted from Joelle's face.

"Look, if you want to get out of here, you're going to have to pretend you never noticed. Do you understand?" she said to Scout. She was standing over Scout now, but not in a threatening way. If anything, she sounded desperate.

"Are you guys doing something that's making the ground shake?" Scout asked. "But what the hell could you be doing that would make the ground shake? Just the seven of you—what could you possibly be doing?"

"It's not us, but that's all I can tell you. Please just drop it," Joelle said. Scout looked over at Bente, who had gone from green to white.

"You're both scared," Scout said, realizing it was true. But of what? The thing making the ground shake, or that Scout might figure out what it was? She shook her head when neither answered her and started toward the door back to the warehouse, but Joelle blocked her path.

"Don't," Joelle said. "Honest, you don't want to dig into this. My father will never let you go if he thinks you even suspect. We don't even talk about it with each other."

"There are other ways out," Scout said. "In one of the corners I didn't explore, or a nook in that cavern that doesn't lead up to the top of the canyon. There's another way out that Tucker didn't show me." Joelle was clutching her own upper arms so tightly her fingers were making blanched circles in her flesh. Scout was getting close to something. "The rats are coming in somehow."

"You want to take your rover with you when you leave, right?" Joelle said. "Then you have to do it my way. Wait for my father. I'll convince him to make the time to talk with you the minute he gets back. I'll see you on your way. You just have to trust me."

Scout wanted to laugh, but she was afraid that if she gave in to that impulse she would be cackling like an unhinged maniac within seconds. Instead, she just scoffed, shaking her head as she turned away.

The dogs fell in step beside her as she walked back out to the open air and bright midafternoon sun, out to where the rover was parked, repaired, and waiting for her.

She had left the door open. It would be hot inside, but she could start up the engines to run the climate controls to cool it off. She lifted Gert inside, Shadow making his own leap to land beside Gert before Scout pulled the door closed.

The air inside was indeed close and hot. Scout moved through the living space to the bottom of the steps leading up to the cockpit. But then she stopped there, hand on the bottom of the rail.

Something was wrong.

She turned back to look at the space behind her. Sink still full of dirty sporks, recycler still overflowing with unprocessed trash, crates everywhere filled with Ottilie's junk. Nothing out of the ordinary.

No, the junk was what was wrong. Scout looked inside one of the crates that sat near the dining table. It looked like it was all still there, but it had been moved. Like someone had dumped it and searched through it, then put it all back.

Scout's stomach suddenly clenched, then went into free fall, and she put a hand out to catch the edge of the table before the rest of her body fell after it. She lifted her eyes to what she had noticed as she had entered the rover but hadn't paid enough attention to.

The hook on the wall near the bunk was empty. The belt, Gertrude's belt, was gone.

Scout broke out into a cold sweat. She couldn't get to the rendezvous without that belt. It wasn't just that she had intended to return all that equipment to Liam when she met him. She had never committed the coordinates to memory, never even entered them in the rover's navigation system. Without the tablet, she didn't know where to go. And she would have no way to send another message to Liam. He would never know why she didn't show.

Had it been there when she had left the rover hours before with Tucker? Scout closed her eyes and tried to recreate that moment, but she simply hadn't been paying attention. The last time she had looked at the belt, she hadn't even really been looking at it.

She had been pointing out her saddlebags to Joelle. The belt had been hanging on the wall just over them. Joelle didn't miss much, and Scout had as good as shown her that she was leaving all of that equipment out, unguarded, free for the taking.

Scout threw the door back open and jumped out of the rover again, the dogs eagerly jumping out after her, barking in the excitement of whatever it was that was happening. Scout burst into the equipment room but had to pause there for her eyes to adjust to the dim interior.

Joelle was standing over one of the control panels but looked up to frown questioningly at Scout scowling at her from the doorway.

"You robbed me," Scout said, her voice a low rumble in her own ears. Strangely, she hadn't been feeling her own anger, but she could hear it. And once she heard it, she realized her hands were in fists and her heart was racing and the blood was singing in her ears.

"Excuse me?" Joelle said, all innocence.

"You took my belt. The one in the rover. The one with all my stuff," Scout said.

"I don't know what you're talking about," Joelle said. She straightened up to her full if petite height, not quelled by Scout's radiating anger as she crossed the room to stand nose to nose with Joelle.

"Give it back," Scout said. "You give it back!"

She might have raised a fist. It was all a blur, but then Bente's hand fell on her shoulder. Scout quickly spun away before the other girl could get a proper grip.

"Don't, Bente," Joelle said as Bente reached for Scout again. "It's all right. We can figure this out."

"Give me the belt back and I'll leave," Scout said.

"We don't have your belt," Joelle said, raising her hands as if imploring Scout to be reasonable, although she didn't dare use those words.

"Someone took it. It must still be here. Find it!" Scout demanded.

"Why would we take your belt?" Joelle said. She sounded sincerely confused.

"I know you saw it when I arrived. It was loaded with tech from the galactic center. Better than your bandit haul, I'm sure."

"I've explained why we hit those trains; you know we're not just thieves. And we definitely didn't steal from you," Joelle said, still striving for calm.

"Someone did," Scout said.

Then the dogs were barking again, running back out into the sunlight. It took a minute for Scout to hear it too past all the barking: the now-familiar sound of the motorcycle engines echoing through the canyon beyond the gate.

"It's just Tucker and Ken," Joelle said.

"How did they get out if your father locked the gate?" Scout asked.

"He has remote access," Joelle said. "When he called to send them out, he remotely opened the gate. They'll have to call him on comms before they get back in."

Indeed, the engines settled into a throbbing rhythm as the bikes stopped outside the gate, waiting. The dogs were going nuts with anticipation.

Scout turned back to Joelle. Either she was being sincere or she was very good at acting sincere. Scout didn't see a way to tell one from the other, but perhaps it didn't matter. She would act like she believed Joelle wanted what was best for Scout and see where things fell.

She leaned in to speak closer to Joelle's ear. "If neither of you took my belt, and I'm guessing Reggie being in virtual school all day rules him out as well, then one of them must have taken it. It was still there when your dad and uncle left this morning. I know it was."

"They wouldn't do it without orders, and if they had orders, I would know," Joelle said. There was a loud buzz and then the grinding sound of the gate opening. The dogs started to run toward it to investigate, but changed their minds as the drone of the bike motors grew louder. Shadow ran to hide under the rover, but Gert sat down in the middle of the canyon nook to wait and see what would happen next.

Scout doubted very much that she was ever going to have anything like this opportunity again. She whistled for the dogs as she ran for the open rover door. The gate was still slowly grinding open, the motorcycle engines revving as they waited for the gap to grow large enough to enter. Joelle was shouting, but Scout couldn't make out the words. She scooped Gert up in her arms and tossed her inside the rover, then pulled herself up as Shadow leapt up beside her.

Joelle was racing to the rover, still shouting words lost to the chopping echoes from the motorcycles. They must be coming inside the gate now. The sound was so loud. Joelle was waving her hands for Scout to wait, but Scout just slammed the door shut and hurled across the room and up the steps to the cockpit.

The motorcycles had slipped in the narrowest possible gap between the doors. Joelle's father had opened it remotely, and no one was wasting any time. Scout was certain the moment the doors fully opened, they would start closing again.

If she didn't get out now, she likely never would.

Scout fired up the engine and gunned the controls into full-speed reverse without even looking behind her. The motorcycles were maneuverable. Ken and Tucker could get out of the way in time.

She hoped. The cameras were still broken; she was driving blind. She locked down the controls so she could stand up and look through the narrow window.

Someone must have raised a warning, or perhaps Joelle's father was even more cautious than she thought, but the doors were already closing. If they latched together and that enormous wheel lock engaged, she would be trapped here.

Trapped with a bunch of people she had just royally pissed off.

Scout braced herself, gripping the backs of both of the seats in the cockpit as the back end of the rover impacted with the closing doors. The dogs yelped in alarm as the rover's growing velocity came to a very sudden halt. But the engines were still going full out, the treads kicking up a cyclone of dust until they had worn their way down to bare rock.

The whine from the gate motor was climbing to sounds she could barely hear but were a torment to the dogs below. Scout felt herself gritting her teeth, gripping the seat backs with her hands as if anything she could physically do would have any effect on the outcome of rover motor versus gateway.

She was nearly pitched down the steep stairway when the rover won. One of the doors had snapped clean away from the canyon wall and gone spinning off to the left, glinting again and again in the afternoon sun before crashing to the canyon floor, disappearing in yet another cloud of dust.

The other door was holding firm, twisting the rover's trajectory. Scout dropped back into the driver's seat to take manual control, keeping the rover between the narrowing walls of the canyon. The low-level cameras were all gone, but she still had two high-top cameras both facing forward. Not ideal, but it would have to be good enough. She didn't have time to stop the rover and bring one of the crates up to sit on like a booster seat so she could see through the window.

How tall had the original settlers been, anyway? They always looked so tiny on the vids in school.

Scout's chuckle had an edge of madness to it. She bit down hard on her lip and forced herself to focus on getting out of the canyon alive.

At least Ken and Bente had repaired the treads. The rover was running as fast and smooth as ever.

Unfortunately, that was nowhere near as fast as Ken and Tucker could manage on their motorcycles. She could hear their engines as they came after her. They were faster, and they also had weapons. Scout wasn't sure if those guns were capable of piercing the rover's armored hull, but she already knew they didn't need those guns to disable her.

Scout bit down on her lip even harder, the coppery taste of blood filling her mouth. She really had only one option. She gripped the yoke more tightly and brought the rover close to the canyon wall on her left. There was a screech and a change in the drone of one of the engines. Either Ken or Tucker had been moving up on her on the left but had changed their mind and fallen back.

She jerked the yoke the other way, bringing the rover up to the wall on the right side. She got a bit closer than she had intended, snapping away a rocky outcrop. She could hear the fragments raining down on the roof of the rover after arcing far up into the air. Now both of the motorcycles had fallen back, but not far enough. They were just pacing along behind her, waiting for their moment.

And it would come soon enough. She was running out of canyon. Soon she would be back out in the open valley between the hill ridges. She could continue to swerve erratically, but would that be enough to keep them away from her long enough to reach Flat Valley?

Scout looked around at everything on the control panel in front of her and in front of the passenger seat, but there didn't seem to be anything remotely like a weapon anywhere. What could she do?

Then she heard one of the motorcycles kick up its speed. She sat as high as she could in the seat, but she still couldn't even see the horizon through the window, only the overly bright sky around her.

Then a blur of motion crossed into one of the camera's views. One of the bikes was roaring past her, turning and then skidding to a halt to face her. The rider pulled off his goggles and tossed his helmet aside.

Tucker. He was daring her to run him over.

For a moment, she wished she was okay with that. But she wasn't. She grabbed the yoke and swerved away. She straightened back out as quickly as she could. The canyon was wider here than before, but she still wasn't out in the open.

There was another roar of a motorcycle speeding past her, and then Ken was whipping around in front of her, blocking her path. She started to swerve around him as well, but Tucker was already back, dark hair rippling in the wind as he rushed to get in front of the rover. Scout pulled on the yoke, turning back the other way.

Ken had something in his hands, something he fiddled with briefly before throwing it at the rover. It clanged against the hull, but nothing exploded or caught fire. What was it? A tracker?

There was a soft whuffing sound, almost lost under the cacophony of the rover engine running as hot as it could and the two motorcycles accelerating as they circled around her somewhere she couldn't see.

Then all the monitors winked out, and the controls turned to stone in her hands. Scout swore out loud as everything fought her. The yoke refused to turn no matter how she strained at it, and the pedals on the floor were locked, immovable. She couldn't slow down, she couldn't stop.

She couldn't even see.

Scout climbed up on the seat to look through the window. She had a momentary view of the world before her, one of those moments that is over in a fraction of a heartbeat and yet stretches on for eternity, a frozen moment like a painting of infinite detail you could fall into forever. The red and yellow dust whirling in delicate eddies through the air, the perfect blue of the sky somehow feeling cold despite the stifling heat of the afternoon.

The canyon wall rushing to meet her. The bands of color were so beautiful. There were so many, such subtle gradations in color from one to the next. The closer she got, the more details she could discern.

She realized she was going to crash into it and felt sad, so sorry that she was going to mar what should be timeless beauty.

Then she did hit it, and her head hit the unbreakable glass she was peering through, and she felt no more.

17

THROUGH THE HAZE of darkness and pain, Scout's awareness sort of pulsed in and out. She knew her dogs were upset; they both seemed to be all over her, nosing and licking and whining. She tried to push herself up from the rover floor, but her arms wouldn't work.

Then the dogs were barking, and voices were arguing, so angry. She tried to speak, to tell them to leave her dogs be, but the few sounds that squeaked out of her throat weren't speech and went unnoticed by whomever the hands belonged to that lifted her up from the floor.

She whimpered at the sound of the motorcycle engine roaring to life. She was lying across the back of the seat, her hat askew and the sun full in her eyes. The roar of the engine, the heat of the motorcycle under her and the sky above her, the stiflingly thick air—it was all too much. Her awareness slipped away.

She came back when the engine stopped. Someone's hands were trying roughly to sit her up, but someone else knocked them away and she was lifted easily in a third person's arms. They were holding her gently like a baby, but although there were other voices around—Joelle's harsh commanding tones, Tucker's snappy responses, Ken's wordier interjections—no voice came from the neck her forehead was pressed against.

At last, she was out of the baking sun. Then she was deeper in the cavernous coolness of the warehouse. The damp, cool air was soothing on her skin.

A door clanged open and Bente—for it could only be silent Bente carrying her—bent to pass through a small doorway and lay her gently on the floor.

Then the door clanged shut again and Scout's eyes at last flew open. She was alone, entirely alone in the dark.

Scout pressed a hand to her throbbing forehead. The hand came back wet and sticky. Pressing it to the wound nearly made her pass out again, but she took slow breaths and focused on staying in the world. Then she pulled herself across the floor until her outstretched hand found the door.

She knocked as loudly as she could, pounding until her knuckles bled, then turning her hand to strike with the fleshier side of her fist. She felt like she was going to puke. She really wanted to stop moving, just let her eyes slide back shut and rest.

But there was one thing in the world she wanted more than that.

She wanted her dogs.

"Dogs!" she shouted, not much louder than her ever-quieter pounding, but it was the most she could say. Her thoughts wouldn't pull together to let her focus on more than that. "Dogs! My dogs!"

Her energy flagged all too quickly, and she slumped to the floor, tears leaking from the corners of her eyes.

She drifted in and out, the aching in her head the only constant in her lightless world. But eventually the bolt in the door clanged open and Scout pushed herself back up on her extended arms, blinking against the dim light shining in at her.

There was a scuffle of dog nails, and then her world was all wet noses and almost painfully coarse paw pads that raked at her. She couldn't summon words, but she managed to put a hand on each of them until they calmed.

"Food for the dogs," Reggie said, setting a bowl on the ground against the wall. "Food for you," he said, putting a wrapped MRE closer to Scout. "And here's a canteen with water. I'm not supposed to talk."

Scout tipped her head back to see him standing at the door. He was alone, and if Scout was capable of getting to her feet, she might be able to take advantage of that fact, to bowl the twelve-year-old to the ground and charge past him, to escape.

But at that moment, all she could do was blink at him over and over, trying and failing to bring his form into clearer focus.

Then the door clanged shut, and he was gone.

The dogs kept licking at Scout. Her head was still throbbing, as was her bruised chest, but they were finding other little injuries all over her. She had gotten scraped up in the crash or during the motorcycle ride back to the compound. But scrapes didn't worry her.

At last, the dogs stopped licking her and settled in close at her sides. They had slept this way through many cold nights out in the open, Shadow in her arms and Gert tucked against the backs of her legs. Their warmth was such a comfort that Scout felt her cheeks getting wet with tears again.

The door clanged open again some time later. Scout opened her eyes, letting Shadow go as he lunged forward to stand between her and the new intruder. Gert stayed close to Scout, and Scout used her for support to pull herself up to a facsimile of a sitting position.

"Hey." It was Ken. "How's your head?"

Scout said not a word.

"One of us should probably bandage that up for you, I guess," he said. "Listen, Malcolm is going to be back here real soon, and it would be really helpful if I could distract him by showing him anything on that belt of yours. It's fantastic tech, right? Only I can't get any of it to do a damn thing. The gun won't even shoot. It can't all be broken. Why would you carry it around if it was all broken? But I've never seen anything like it, any of it. I can't even find the on switches or anything? Can you help me out?"

Scout still didn't speak.

"Yeah, I get it," Ken said. "I guess you were pretty mad that I took it. Malcolm wanted me to take a look at your stuff when you weren't around and grab anything that looked useful. I couldn't exactly ask you first or anything. I know you hate it here, I get it, but you don't know what it was like out there. I mean, I guess you think you do?

Because you heard stories? But you don't really know. And yeah, it's getting kinda scary in here too, but it's still better than out there. So if I say I'd do anything Malcolm asks me, don't give me that look like I joined some sort of cult or whatever, because it's not like that. I know what he's asking and why. War is coming, and anything we can do to fight that, it's got to be a good thing, right?"

Scout rested her chin on Gert's head. This conversation was exhausting.

"I guess you don't see it that way. Fine. I'm sure I can figure something out. It's just, if you helped out before Malcolm came back, he's more likely to put you in the friend than foe category. And you really don't want to be in his foe category. We're all trying to keep you out of that, if you would just cooperate?"

Scout was finding it harder to stay sitting. At least Gert didn't mind Scout slumping over her. She was a strong dog.

"I'll see about that bandage," Ken said, getting to his feet. He noticed the untouched food and lifted the canteen to feel the weight of the untouched water inside. Then he went back out the door.

Shadow came back to her and Scout was sorely tempted to lie down and go back to sleep, but she couldn't.

She had to get out of this place. The day must be gone now, or nearly so. Which meant this was her last night. She had to get to the rendezvous before morning. She had to get moving.

Scout reached for the canteen and took a few cautious sips. The pukey feeling was gone, anyway. She wet the corner of her shirt and cleaned her face as well as she could in the dark with no mirror. Then she opened the MRE and ate whatever was inside. Synthesized meat of some sort in a tomato sauce. Not remotely like her last dinner or even the breakfast she had only picked at.

The food gone, she felt a touch better. She felt around the room, but the only other object besides the canteen was the bowl of food the dogs had consumed while she had slept. She took an inventory of what she had on her.

Her hat was gone. That started a flame of anger in her heart. Her father had given her that hat.

She still had her sun-protective shirt on over her tank top. That was good. She might still need that.

Cargo shorts, socks, and boots all accounted for. The belt, of course, was gone.

Scout got up on her knees and thrust her hands into her various pockets. The thigh pocket on the right was still filled with round stones, the slingshot in her left hip pocket, although the utility knife was gone. The other hip and thigh pockets were empty. She tried the front pocket.

The data disks were nestled still against her left hip. That was good. She withdrew her hand without them. She didn't know if anyone was watching her, but better safe than sorry.

Then her fingertips brushed against something in her right front pocket and she froze, not wanting to pull it out either, not wanting to risk it being seen.

Gertrude's lens. No wonder Ken couldn't make heads or tails of the equipment on the belt. None of it worked at all without the lens. The lens made the controls visible, allowed them to function. The right lens had been shattered when Gertrude had died, but Scout had managed to operate what she needed with just the left lens.

The door opened again. Scout sat back on her heels just before Joelle came into view, holding a first aid kit in one hand and with an electric lantern dangling from its handle between her teeth as she used her other hand to close the door behind her.

"How's your head?" Joelle asked as she leaned in with the lantern now in her hand to look. Scout flinched away from the too-bright light. Joelle changed the angle of the light, still examining the wound. Then she set the lantern down and opened the first aid kit, digging through it until she found a tube of cream.

"It looks like you cleaned it up all right," Joelle said as she squeezed a line of white cream across her fingertips. "This is antibacterial. It doesn't really sting." She grabbed Scout's arm anyway, as if she might pull away, then gently spread the cream over the split lump above Scout's right eyebrow. "I see your food's gone," she said as she dug through the kit again for a bandage. "Are you still hungry?"

"What time is it?" Scout asked. Her voice was raspy, as if she hadn't used it in weeks.

"Just past sunset," Joelle said, her attention focused above Scout's eyes as she carefully dressed the wound. "My father should be back soon."

"Then what?" Scout asked.

"Then I don't know," Joelle said. "You've made things complicated."

Scout made a sound somewhere between a laugh and a cough. "*I* made?"

"You've put me in a very difficult position, yes," Joelle said. "I know you didn't ask to come here, that Tucker dragged you here. And I know my father freaked you out this morning. But what you don't get is that I'm trying to help you. And you keep making it difficult."

"You should probably stop trying to help me then," Scout said.

Joelle sat back and looked her right in the eye. "No," Joelle said. "You don't want to know how things will go for you without me helping. You really don't."

Scout didn't know how to answer that. Before she could summon any words at all, Joelle was gone, taking the first aid kit and the lantern with her.

Scout was once more alone with her dogs in the dark. But at least night had only just begun. She still had time to figure something out.

Scout ran her hands over every centimeter of the walls and over every bit of the earthen floor. She traced every part of the door with her fingertips. She even jumped again and again, brushing her hands over the low ceiling that hung featureless over her.

There was nothing. Not one usable thing.

At last, Scout curled up once more with her dogs and waited. There was nothing else she could do.

She woke from a fitful doze to the sound of the door once more clanging open. Someone stepped inside, from darkness to darkness. Scout could hear breathing, but nothing else. She sat up and crept back until she felt the wall behind her.

The dogs sensed her fear, and both rose up, backs bristling as they growled. Had enough time passed for Joelle's father to return? Was he in the little cell with her?

"Hey, calm your dogs down," Tucker said from the darkness.

"I don't think so," Scout said. "I don't think I feel like calm is the answer to anything just now."

"Hold on," Tucker said, and she could hear him fumbling with something. Then there was a little light, glowing redly from between his cupped palms at first, but with a more yellowish glow as he set it down on the ground. Some sort of pocket lantern, just an exposed bulb on a tiny stand. He was on his knees but sat back on his heels once he had the light glowing. Then he held something up in his hand to show her.

"Jolo," Scout said, recognizing the bottle. The unmistakable bottle. The one great obsession in her life.

"You like?" Tucker asked, then pulled off the cap. There was a hiss of escaping carbonation and Scout's mouth immediately began to water. That was just what she needed, here in this place. A massive dose of sugar and caffeine, enough to keep her wakeful through the rest of the night, however much remained.

"I like," she said, reaching out for the bottle. He handed it to her with a smile. Then, once she took it from him, he moved to sit not exactly beside her but with his back against the same wall.

Scout took a long pull from the bottle. The sugar raced right to her brain, making every nerve cell sing like a choir of angels. The caffeine was still in her blood, spreading through her body, promising to perk up every bit of her in just a few blinks of an eye.

"It's in short supply around here, but I'm pretty good with thieving when I have to be," Tucker said, then held his hand out to her. She handed the bottle back, and he took a quick sip. "Yep, just as good as I remembered."

"Good at thieving, huh?" Scout said. He handed the bottle back to her, and she wiped the opening with the edge of her shirt before taking another drink.

"Hey, it was Ken who took your stuff. He promised he'd fess up."

"He did," Scout said as the second rush of sugar washed over her brain.

"I'm sorry about all of this," Tucker said, moving closer to her as she handed him back the bottle. Shadow was between them and growled without lifting his head, a sort of proximity warning. Gert was across the room examining the empty food bowl.

"You should be," Scout said as unkindly as she could.

"I know, I know," he said, taking another sip, then handing her back the bottle.

"What time is it?" Scout asked.

"Nearly dawn. Maybe an hour 'til."

Scout looked at the bottle in her hands and took another drink. "And Joelle's father?"

"He's here. He's got a lot on his mind at the moment. Frankly, it's better for you if he forgets you're here for a little bit. We'll keep you fed and all that, no worries, but we should give him a few days to deal with some other issues before he gets to the issue of you."

"I can't do that," Scout said. "I have a place to be. I only have a little bit of time left to get there. I *have* to go."

"Sounds serious," Tucker said, taking the bottle of jolo from her hands. "Are you in trouble?"

"No, it's not that," Scout said. He looked relieved at her answer. The jolo was mostly gone, and he had to tip his head back to take another drink. Scout watched his throat move as he swallowed. It was strangely fascinating. Perhaps that was the head injury talking. He left the last bit in the bottle when he handed it back to her, then dried his lips on the back of his sleeve as he watched her drink the last of the fizzy goodness.

"What is it?" he asked. He tried to move closer to her again, and Shadow gave another low growl. Scout put her hand under his hind end and gently encouraged him to join Gert at licking the last of the long-gone flavor from the sides of the food bowl.

"Can I tell you?" she asked, looking over at him. He was very close now, his sleeve almost brushing hers. She fixed her attention back on the now-empty bottle, turning it over and over in her hands.

"You can tell me anything," he said. "You were going to tell me something before, weren't you?"

Scout said nothing, just kept her focus on the bottle. She felt weird, floaty, like she wasn't really there or was perhaps too much there. It wasn't that bottle-of-jolo-on-an-empty-stomach feeling; she knew that one well. And the throbbing had stopped hours before, so she didn't think it was from the bump on her head. But something was definitely different.

"Do you want me to guess?" he asked, and his hands slid over hers, following the lines of her fingers to gently slip the bottle away and set it aside. "You're going away. Far, far away. You're going to escape, not just this room, but this whole world. Am I right?"

She swallowed back that strange feeling and looked up at him. How had he gotten so close? Their noses were almost touching. "Yes," she said. His hands were back on hers, so warm. Hers were still icy from clutching that bottle.

"Were you going to ask me to come with you?" His voice was teasing, but his eyes were deadly serious.

"If I did, what would you say?" she asked. She swallowed again; her throat felt so thick.

He smiled. Not the same smile he had kept unleashing on her since they met, the smile that was so eager for her to smile back, too eager. This one was smaller, more genuine.

Well, smaller on his lips. But bigger in that it extended to his eyes.

"Is that a yes?" Scout asked, but the end of the last word never quite made it out into the world. His lips were on hers and all the words died.

His hands touched her hair, her face, her arms. She felt like she was floating, but floating down, drifting down to the ground like driftwood flowing with the current of a river. She held on to him to keep her equilibrium, his shoulders and his arms.

He smelled indescribably good. He tasted like jolo, a cool, tangy zing to each of his kisses. One of his hands slipped back up to touch her cheek with infinite tenderness, like he adored her beyond words and could express it only through this touch.

His other hand slipped down her hip.

No, not her hip. He was in her pocket.

Scout broke the kiss, shoving both forearms between them and pushing him away, but too late. He rolled away from her, holding something in his hand close to the light from the little lantern. His back was to her. She couldn't see what he was examining, but she didn't need to. She felt the cold absence of those two little data disks from her pocket.

"No!" she said, lunging for him, but he slipped from her grasp. He stopped in the doorway for a moment, not looking back at her.

"Malcolm needs this," he said, as if that explained everything.

Then he was gone.

Scout pounded her already-bruised fists on the hatch and shrieked until her throat gave out, but there was no bringing him back.

Oh, she had been stupid. So very stupid. And now she had lost everything.

18

SCOUT SAT with her back against the door, her head in her hands. The rush of sugar and caffeine was fading, but not before reawakening the throbbing pain over her eye. Her hands throbbed as well from pounding ineffectually at the door. Even the spot on her chest where that kid had hit her with a rock two days ago was making itself felt again.

She heard the dogs snuffling about in the corners of the room and guessed she was going to have some fun new smells to go with the aches and pains in just a few minutes. And if nobody let her out soon, she was going to have to contribute to the smells herself.

Scout tipped her head back to gently rap it against the door behind her. How could she have been so stupid? She couldn't even work out the exact moment when she had just decided to trust Tucker. The idea that she had never decided, that it had just happened, bothered her more. How could she have *let* it happen?

But how had he known she even had those disks? She had never mentioned them. She had resisted the temptation to touch them. Had he discerned their shape through the faded khaki of her shorts?

But then, had he even known what he was taking? He must have known. The way he had looked at them before leaving the cell, very cursory, like he was just making sure. Not like he was examining some strange thing he had happened to find.

They knew she had been there, where Ruth had died. They hadn't found what they were looking for in the town car or in the remains of the way station or in the rover when they had searched it. So they had deduced that it had to be on her person. That had to be what happened.

Scout groaned aloud and rapped her head against the door again. How could they have searched the way station so quickly? It wasn't possible. Perhaps they had decided to search her to be sure and, sure enough, had found what they were looking for.

Unless… what was the faster search method Bente had used on the town car? And had Tucker and Ken's mission been to bring this… whatever to Malcolm and Arvid so they could use it on the station?

It seemed likely she'd never know.

It would be too much to hope they wouldn't have any more luck than she had reading what was on those disks. At least one of them had been meant to be read by them, the rebels, at some point.

The snuffling in the corner was growing more persistent and Scout crawled closer to see what the dogs were up to. Had they smelled something? Gert was making that whining noise she always made when her prey was out of reach. Slowly, Scout realized she could see. Not much, but the faintest of lights was outlining the dogs' heads, making Shadow's white fur shine ever so softly.

They were digging in the corner, getting increasingly excited. They had smelled something, had found something.

A way out.

Scout crawled in between the two of them, both frantically digging. Yes, there was something, a vent so low the packed earth of the floor had completely covered it. Scout tried to help dig, but the dogs were much more efficient than she was, and she sat back out of the way until they had the vent entirely uncovered.

Whatever the dogs were smelling on the far side of the vent was driving them mad. Gert dug at the metal and Shadow tried pulling it apart with his teeth, but it was no good. They couldn't pry it away.

Scout leaned in. With the light coming from the other side, it was hard to make out the details of how the vent was attached, but her fingertips felt the heads of four screws holding the vent tight against the wall.

She checked her pockets again, but the only thing she still had on her was Gertrude's lens. It was too delicate to use as a tool to remove the vent; she would just end up shattering the lens. She tried using her nails, but even after ripping each to the quick, she had not so much as loosened the first screw.

She needed something metallic.

Her zipper.

Scout quickly pulled off her shorts and grasped the tag of her zipper in her bloody fingers. It was small, but it might work. The first turn was the hardest, but after a few rotations, there was enough of the first screwhead exposed to continue unscrewing it with her fingers.

The dogs saw what she was doing and started pawing at the vent again, anxious to get through. This made it harder to work, but Scout persevered, removing the other three screws one by one. Then she stepped back and let the dogs go at it.

The vent still refused to move.

Scout tried digging her fingertips around the edges but couldn't get a hold anywhere.

The dogs were whining, as frustrated as she was. Scout laid down on the floor and started kicking at the vent with both legs, over and over. Finally, the vent dented in the middle and broke away from the wall. One more kick and it was completely free, spinning through the air to land somewhere in the far corner of the room.

"Yes!" Scout cried. There was a tussle as the dogs both tried to go through at once, but Shadow, being smaller, slipped ahead. The glow of his white fur grew as he crawled. Then Gert blocked Scout's view with her big black body and Scout was once more alone in the dark.

Scout pulled her shorts back on, then poked her head inside the hole. She could just fit through the opening in the wall, but the vent beyond was not squared off and regular like a proper vent. It looked more like a wormhole tunneling through the rock. It was wider just beyond the wall, but what if it got narrower again further in?

How far did it go? There was light ahead of her again, but no sign of the dogs. They had turned a corner, but either the tunnel got larger or they were out of it entirely because their bodies were no longer blocking the light.

She couldn't tell if it got narrower or not. She wouldn't know until she tried. But what if Scout tried to follow the dogs and got stuck?

Then again, the alternative was to wait in this room until her captors decided how to dispose of her.

Scout had just put her head and shoulders inside the hole when the dogs ahead of her started barking. Scout gripped with her bloody fingertips and pulled herself along the tunnel as quickly as she could, pushing with her toes but not having enough room to use her knees. She wiggled as fast as she could, but she was all too aware of how slow that was.

Her dogs needed her. She wriggled faster.

Then she got stuck. She was almost at the point where the tunnel took a turn to the left, but she wasn't close enough to it to see anything. She reached out and grabbed the largest outcropping of rock she could find, but it still wasn't large enough for her to grasp it with her hand.

The flesh on the ends of her fingers was going to be completely gone before she got out of this hole.

If she got out at all. Her hips were caught, and no matter how she pulled or twisted, she couldn't get free.

And her dogs were calling for her.

Scout screamed in her frustration, screamed until her lungs were empty, then kicked and pulled.

It did no good. She was stuck. She put her head down to cry but bumped the sore spot hard enough to see stars.

Something was scuffling toward her through the tunnel, blocking off the light. The dogs were still barking like mad, but the sound was muffled. Whatever they had been barking at had gotten past them and was coming for Scout.

She tried moving backwards, but that was impossible. Her flesh was starting to swell up all around her hips. That wasn't helping.

Then someone clasped one of her out-flung hands. Not like they were capturing it, more like giving her a gentle squeeze to lend her strength.

"Hey, Scout." A young voice. Reggie. "Why didn't you follow the dogs?"

"I'm stuck," Scout said, squirming.

"Oh. Well, just lie still for a minute. I'm going to go get something."

Then he was gone. Scout held her breath, straining to hear what was going on. Was he going to help her or to tell his sister about her escape attempt?

The light dimmed and was eclipsed before she heard the sound of Reggie returning.

"Where are the dogs?" Scout asked as he crawled nearer.

"They're back in the cave behind me, eating. I brought water for them too," he said.

"What are you doing in a cave?" Scout asked.

"Trying to get you out," Reggie said, then, "take this. It's a stone file. If you can get it between your body and the sides of the tunnel, you can probably file off enough of the stone to get through. It's pretty crumbly here."

Scout took the long, flat metal tool and felt the end of it with her fingertips. It was smooth on one side but rough on the other, with metal nubs sharp enough to prick at her hands. She squirmed a bit, then found a place where she could force it past the back of her hip and file away at one of the rocky protrusions.

"Thanks for the help," Scout said as she worked. "But what brought you down here in the first place?"

"Like I said, to get you out," Reggie said. "Joelle sent me. She knew about this tunnel, but there wasn't any way to tell you about it. The cell is monitored. I mean, only Ken is watching most of the time, but when one of us goes in there, my dad watches the whole time. So we couldn't tell you about the buried vent. Then I remembered something about dogs. It took a while to make what I needed. Good thing I've been learning how to print plastics for one of my classes, and that we had a printer in the warehouse. Otherwise, I don't know how I would have ever found one."

"One what?" Scout asked, gritting her teeth as the file ground against her hipbone. It was working, though; she was nearly free.

"A dog whistle," Reggie said. "Dogs can hear it, but people can't.

The security system's audio pickups might register it, but they wouldn't trigger an alert. So if someone goes back later, they might hear me whistling, but for now no one knows. I mean, Ken would have seen the dogs and you escaping, but he's been running old footage on his monitor, so if my dad goes to check, everything looks normal. So no one knows you're here."

"Except Joelle," Scout said, pulling the file back out in front of her and handing it back to Reggie.

"Except me and Joelle," he agreed. "Can you come out now?"

Scout grasped the tunnel walls as firmly as she could with her aching fingertips, then tucked the toes of her boots as far up as she could and strained with everything to pull herself forward.

The stone all around her clung to her hips, but she pulled herself through. She didn't want to think about the condition of her shorts; she had heard the rending of fabric and could feel the throbbing of abrasions on her thighs. But that didn't matter; she was free.

"Come on," Reggie said, crawling backwards faster than she could follow going forwards. Her foot bumped something. She realized it was her slingshot, which had fallen when her back pocket had been torn away. She kicked it forward, not far enough to reach with her hands but enough to keep kicking it along the tunnel as she crawled.

The tunnel widened just after the turn, and she could reach a hand back and grasp the slingshot. Then she could get up on her elbows and knees, then her hands and knees, and then she was out of the tunnel, standing trembly legged and dusty in what looked like the bottom of a well, lit up by an electric lantern in the middle of the space. She put the slingshot in her other pocket as she looked around. She tipped her head back, but the ceiling was lost in shadows far above her. The walls around her glittered in the electric light, rock formations like frozen waterfalls cascading all around her. It was so beautiful her breath caught.

Shadow and Gert looked up from their feast to see her standing there and belatedly charged over to greet her. Reggie watched the three of them with a big grin on his face.

"Where are we?" Scout asked.

"Under the warehouse," Reggie said. "This place was an abandoned mine when my father found it. We mostly only use the office space upstairs, but it goes down forever in a maze of mined tunnels and natural caverns."

"Tucker skipped that bit when he gave me the tour," Scout said.

"Technically, all of this is off-limits to us," Reggie said. "My dad walled it off, but there is an access panel. Joelle found it years ago. He doesn't know we know."

"You're going to get in trouble for this," Scout guessed.

"Only if we get caught," Reggie said, flashing that grin again.

"Eventually they'll notice I'm gone."

"No worries. Joelle is keeping my dad distracted upstairs, and I'm supposed to be sleeping for a few hours yet, so no one is going to notice I'm not there. I'm going to get you and the dogs out and be back before breakfast. It will look like you found your own way out and no one will be the wiser."

"I don't want to get you in trouble," Scout said, "but I also can't just leave without my things."

"The rover is smashed," Reggie said. "It was too big to try to tow back, so the others left it in the canyon. You can get inside it, but I'd guess by now the bandits have found it. They'll take whatever they can find. They'll even strip it for parts if they can't move it."

"I don't need the rover," Scout said. "Ken stole my equipment belt. I need that back. I can't leave without it."

"I can't get it for you," Reggie said with a frown. "I don't think even Joelle could get it. It's too dangerous."

"I have to have it. I literally can't leave without it. If I don't have it, I might as well go back into that cell."

"Seriously?" Reggie said. He looked distraught at this glitch in his escape plan. "I can try to ask Joelle what to do—"

"It's not just that," Scout said. "Tucker took some disks from me. I need those as well."

"I don't know anything about that," Reggie said. "I don't know what to do."

"Don't worry about it. I'll figure something out," Scout said. "This was a good plan, to make it look like I escaped. That doesn't have to change. What were you going to do next?"

"There is a tunnel that goes under the canyon behind the compound," Reggie said. "It was part of the mine. It comes out on the far side, out of sight from the top of the ridge here. You could come out of that end in the full light of day and no one here would know."

"Can you still show me that tunnel? Where it starts on this end?" Scout asked.

"Sure," Reggie said. "It's a straight run, easy to follow because every wrong turn is a natural cavern, not squared off like the tunnel. You can't possibly get lost. Plus, this lantern is for you. I have a pocket light to get back with."

"Show me where the tunnel starts, then show me how to get back into the compound," Scout said. "Then you go back to bed; I don't want you or Joelle to get into trouble for helping me out. If I get caught, it will look like I escaped on my own."

"But Scout, if you go back, you *will* get caught," Reggie said. "There's no way you won't."

"I'll take the chance," Scout said. "I can't leave without that belt."

Reggie nodded glumly and picked up the lantern to lead the way. The dogs, who had been licking all around the entirely empty food bowl in search of possible remaining crumbs, immediately ran to follow him. Scout trailed behind, the throbbing of her head worse now that she was standing up and moving about rather than resting.

She couldn't let that stop her. She had to get that belt back. She wanted the disks too if she could manage it.

And if she should encounter Tucker again? That would be a nice bonus. She wanted a better ending between them than the one he had just given her. And she could think of so many better endings. Endings only she walked away from.

19

SCOUT HAD THOUGHT the painted walls of the canyon exterior were lovely, but every cavern Reggie guided her through was its own wonderland of dazzling sights. In one room, all the rocks were like dazzling diamonds winking whitely in the light from Reggie's lantern; in the next, each rock was its own unique color, all piled together as if some giant had collected them from far-flung regions and then had forgotten them here. Many of the chambers were shaped like deep wells just like the first cavern she had crawled into, but others were like snaky channels hollowed out around larger, impenetrable masses of stone or were wider open spaces but with a ceiling so low even Reggie had to stoop to cross it.

Each cavern took them deeper into the ground, further from the compound, and Scout's mental map got twisted beyond usability.

Then he guided her up another winding channel between rock faces so steep she had to use hands and feet to climb it. By the time she reached the top, she was quite out of breath. Her whole body hurt. It had been a rough few days.

"How much further?" she asked. "I don't remember coming this far when Bente brought me to the cell."

"She didn't," Reggie said, also fighting to catch his breath. "The cell is behind a hidden door at the back of the warehouse. The caves don't run in a straight line. Don't worry; you won't be coming back this way. Not unless you want to go back to your cell through the vent."

"No," Scout said. "For one, I doubt I could fit back through."

Reggie grinned at her, but the smile froze on his face as the ground beneath them began to shake. He reached out a hand to grasp the wall beside him, his eyes wide with fright. The dogs started barking in alarm and ran off into the darkness.

Scout put her arms over her head. The vision of the stone ceiling coming crashing down on her wouldn't leave her mind. Surely if that were likely to happen, it would have already. This made how many quakes now? And surely there had been more before she ventured into this part of the planet.

But this quake felt stronger than the others. Stronger and steadier. Almost rhythmic. And so loud.

Scout dropped her arms, straining to hear. Stones were sliding and falling down the serpentine path behind her, echoing over and over through the caverns, but she thought she could hear something else buried under that racket. Something like an engine. Or a train.

Then the quaking faded away. Reggie gulped, but let go of the wall.

"That happens a lot?" Scout asked.

"More lately," he admitted.

"What is it?" she asked.

"I don't even *know*," he said, annoyed. "Nobody will tell me. But Dad has been a lot more upset since it started happening."

"Angry or scared?" Scout asked.

Reggie considered his answer carefully. "I think both."

"Does Joelle know what this is?"

"If anyone besides my dad and Arvid know, it would be Joelle. But Dad has been keeping more secrets from her too, so I don't know."

"Did it sound like a machine to you? Or a vehicle of some sort?"

Reggie rolled his eyes up and to the right as he considered. "I don't know," he said. "I want to hear it again."

"We need to get moving," Scout said, and Reggie nodded. "Where are the dogs?" She didn't wait for an answer, just whistled the shrill whistle that would always summon the dogs no matter how interesting a distraction they had found in the tall prairie grasses that were their usual haunt.

This time there was no pattering sound of returning paws.

Reggie tried his plastic whistle. Scout heard only the soft sound of his breath passing through it. They waited for several long moments, but still the dogs didn't return.

"The cavern opens up ahead just where it meets the mining tunnel. They might be there," Reggie said. "Everything echoes here, but up there the space kind of swallows up all sounds."

"Show me," Scout said. The dogs had run ahead, but she was very afraid they would take a different turn, perhaps through a space too small for even Reggie to follow them. What if they got lost? Or worse, separated and lost? What if they couldn't find their way back to her? She couldn't just leave them down here to die alone in the dark, but how could she ever search such an immense, twisting labyrinth?

"It's here," Reggie said, ducking under a low-hanging rock. The space beyond really did seem to be snatching the words away the moment they left his mouth. It was like the opposite of an echo; Scout didn't like it.

Scout ducked under the same rock and found herself standing on a ledge with a long drop before her. Reggie was standing at the edge, shining the lantern over the side. She stepped up beside him, but his light wasn't strong enough to reach the bottom or whatever was on the far side of the chasm. It was like standing at the edge of one of the canyons above, only this one was hidden underground. Reggie didn't look concerned with the size of the space, though. He was only shining his light straight down, as if searching for something.

"Scout, what if they fell in the quake?" Reggie asked, no more than a whisper. Scout swallowed hard; she had been thinking the same thing.

"Both together? Without crying out? I don't think so," she said, although she was far from sure. She caught Reggie's hand and gave it a squeeze. "They'll be okay."

"Yes, I think you're right," Reggie said.

"What's down there?" Scout asked.

"I don't know. I always kind of hurry past this bit," Reggie admitted. "It feels too much like something is sleeping down there, some enormous monster. Something you never, ever want to wake up. I mean, obviously I know there isn't."

"I get you," Scout said. "I wouldn't want to go down there either. The air feels strange." She held out her hands, fingers spread wide. It was clammier here, and there was a definite cold breeze moving past them. How far did this cavern run?

Reggie was just about to speak again when they both froze at the sudden sound of angry barking. Both of the dogs were in high alert mode—not behind them in the labyrinth, and thankfully not down in the immense cavern, but further on the way Reggie had been leading her.

Reggie raised the lantern high as they both jogged along the sandy ledge as it widened and then expanded out into another natural cavern. The far side of the cavern ended in a squared-off mining tunnel, the opening outlined in dim red lights.

They found the dogs on the right side of the cavern, barking at something behind a forest of stalactites that Scout couldn't see. Shadow was bristling all over, every muscle in his little body tense as he crouched low and barked and even snarled. The black hair on Gert's back was raised up in a ridge that made her seem even larger than she already was, and her deep barks echoed painfully through the chamber.

"What is it?" Reggie asked. "Not a rat."

"Oh, it's a rat all right," Scout said as she drew close enough to see Tucker trying desperately to balance on the top of a boulder. One foot kept slipping over the wet surface, finally slipping enough for Gert to lunge in and take a chomp at it.

"Call off the dogs!" Tucker wailed.

"No," Scout said, crossing her arms. "I really don't think so."

"This isn't good," Reggie said, close at her elbow. "If he's here, they know you're gone."

"No one else knows yet, but please call off the dogs!" Tucker said, nearly toppling off his precarious perch. "Someone is going to hear them."

Scout frowned. He had a point. "Shadow, Gert, come!"

Shadow was at her side in a flash, albeit still growling low in his throat and standing at attention. She had to call Gert's name twice more before the dog would stop trying to climb up the side of the boulder after Tucker. His foot kept almost slipping back into her reach and walking away from that was hard for an untrained puppy. But Scout put all the command she could into calling one last time and Gert reluctantly obeyed.

"Thank you!" Tucker said. He was looking quite pale, but Scout felt no pity. His dog fear had a way of waxing and waning to whatever level was convenient for him. She wasn't going to indulge him by taking it seriously.

"Don't thank me," Scout said. "I'm just thinking it would be quieter to drag you down from that rock and throw you down the hole back there."

"You don't want to do that," Tucker said. "I'm here to help."

"Help me what? Reggie already busted me out," Scout said.

"If you let me talk to you, I can explain everything," he said. "Please, just have Reggie take the dogs away for a moment. I just need a moment. Please?"

Scout closed her eyes to the sight of him pleading with her, his face contorted in what really looked like sincere regret and desire for the chance to make it up to her. She turned to Reggie.

"What do you think?" she asked.

"Me?" he asked, hand on his chest.

"Yeah," Scout said. She supposed not many people around here asked the littlest kid what he thought about anything. "You've known Tucker a lot longer than I have. And I believe you have my best interests at heart. Mine and the dogs'. So, what do you think? Do I trust him?"

Reggie looked at Tucker as if seeing him for the first time. Tucker kept silent as the twelve-year-old thought carefully before answering. "I'll hold the dogs," he said at last. "But I'm not going away. We'll be right here where I can let them go again if he tries anything."

"So you don't trust him?" Scout asked. She was surprised to find herself surprised by that.

"I'm not sure," Reggie said. "Most times he's cool. He lets me help with stuff and seems like a great guy."

"I *am* a great guy," Tucker said, but he fell silent again at Scout's sharp glare.

"But other times?" she prompted Reggie.

The boy looked up at Tucker, then moved closer to Scout to speak too low for Tucker to hear. "It's just a feeling I have. Sometimes I think he makes trouble between my sister and my dad. Not enough where anyone could ever say it's his fault. Not enough where I can even tell Joelle about it, because I have no proof, just a feeling. I think he thinks he should be in charge when the grown-ups are away, not my sister, but I don't think he should. And no, I don't trust him."

Scout put a hand on his shoulder. "Thanks for that."

"No problem," he said. It was too dark in the cavern to tell for sure, but Scout just knew he was blushing. He knelt down, putting an arm around each dog and hugging them tight to his sides.

Scout turned to face Tucker, who slid down from the boulder, brushing clammy grit from his hands as he walked up to her. If he was bothered by not having heard exactly what Reggie had said to her, he didn't show it.

In fact, he was smiling at her again, that maddening smile that was always looking for a response. She had no qualms about not returning it. She did, however, take a deliberate step back when he tried to get within arm's reach of her. A step closer to her dogs. Tucker stopped moving, hands raised to show he meant no harm.

"Talk from there," Scout said, crossing her arms once more.

"Sure," Tucker said. He kept glancing past her at the listening Reggie, and she was sure he would have preferred to talk to her alone but apparently knew better than to ask. There was no way she was stepping away from her dogs now. "Listen, did you even know what you were carrying?" His gray eyes were shining brightly, and Scout felt her heart sink. Whatever was on those disks, they had it now. And apparently it was killer.

"Did *you* know?" she countered.

"No," Tucker said. "No, I didn't know you had anything. Malcolm figured out you must have taken what he was looking for. I mean, you were there when Ruth died, right?"

Scout said nothing, only nodded.

"I thought so. There were a lot of bodies down there," he added, looking up at her through his lashes. She just stared at him stonily until he went on. "Malcolm was going to search you. Thoroughly. Do you follow? It wouldn't have been pleasant."

Scout barked out a humorless laugh, then turned away until she had blinked away the prickly feeling she wasn't going to let become tears. "You had a more pleasant option, I guess."

"It was the best I could do on short notice," he said. "I mean, I was pretty sure just asking you wouldn't have led to anything."

Reggie was looking up at Scout, brows furrowed as he tried to guess what they were not quite saying. She raised her chin a bit to let him know she was all right, then turned back to Tucker.

"What was on the disks?" she asked.

"The one you got from Ruth had what Malcolm has been looking for for quite some time," Tucker said. "Design specifications for the big gun and proof that the Space Farers are dismantling the magnetic shield."

Scout blinked, this time in surprise. "Wait, what?"

"Which part?" Tucker asked.

"Both!" Scout said. "So you already knew they were taking down the shield? You acted like I was imagining conspiracies when I brought it up."

"Malcolm suspected," Tucker said. "But now we have proof. We can warn everyone. People down here have a right to know."

"It will mean war," Scout said. "More asteroids falling on cities."

"Maybe not," Tucker said.

"Because there's a big gun?"

"A very big gun," Tucker said, and this time when he took a step closer to her, she didn't step back, although she put clear warning in her eyes. "It's a secret Planet Dweller project. It's why the governor has been saying some of the things he's been saying."

"He's trying to provoke a war?" Scout asked.

"I think he started shooting his mouth off too soon," Tucker said.

"The gun isn't assembled yet, and it seems like the construction fell behind schedule. That's why he's been quieter lately."

"I didn't notice," Scout said, but then she wouldn't have. Up until six days ago, she had never had much interest in politics. Now there was little else she could think about.

"He did, but he's going to start ramping up again, I guarantee it."

Scout felt a cold chill run up her spine. She looked back over her shoulder, past Reggie holding her dogs to the vast cavern beyond. "Is it...?"

"You can't see from up here, but if you went to the bottom, you'd see an immense railway. Truly enormous; the rails are taller than Bente."

"A railway to where?"

"It runs from the closest city, Jakart, to the mountain range to the north."

"All underground?" Scout asked.

"It was part of the mines, once upon a time," Tucker said. "It fell into disuse decades ago, but after the last war Malcolm heard rumors about its existence. Rumors of what the governor was now using it for."

"What?" Scout asked.

"They are building a gun up in the mountains," Tucker said. "They machine the parts in Jakart, then bring them north on the mining railway. They're assembling it inside the tallest mountain, but the mouth of the gun is already aimed for the region of high atmosphere where the Space Farer space stations pass. Once it's ready, they just have to fire. If they pick the right moment, they can take out two-thirds of the population in space in one shot."

"How do you know this?" Scout asked.

"They did the math. It's all on the disk you've been carrying in your pocket," Tucker said, then leaned closer to her ear. "You really had no idea?"

Scout pulled away from him. Was he testing her again? Was he still pumping her for yet more information?

"Hey," he said, reading her thoughts off her face.

"What was on the other disk?" she demanded.

"Census data," he said.

"Census data?" It sounded so dry, and yet his eyes were gleaming again. "That wasn't from Ruth, it was from a different woman."

"We know which one," Tucker said. "Liv something, right? We've been watching her for some time."

"It's a shame she's dead. I'm sure she'd have been gratified to know that," Scout said with as much disdain as she could muster. "What good is census data?"

"It's real," Tucker said. "As opposed to fake, like the data the Space Farers have been sending the governor since the war. They've been inflating their numbers to demand a larger piece of the harvest."

"Inflating."

"Tripling."

Scout gave a low whistle. "People have been going hungry to meet those quotas."

"In case the magnetic shield thing isn't excuse enough for war," Tucker said.

"I don't want war," Scout said, and the smile dropped from his face.

"No one wants war," he said.

"Really? You seem to."

"That's Malcolm."

"You don't want what Malcolm wants?" Scout demanded. "You seem pretty eager to do every little thing that Malcolm tells you to do."

"I want justice," he said, practically spitting the word out. "Don't you? For your family?"

"War won't bring them back," Scout said. "It's just going to destroy more families, and for what? Both sides are wrong here. You do see that, don't you? Both sides are wrong."

"Only one side dropped a rock on my family," Tucker said. "And yours."

Scout turned away from him, looking down at her dogs. Maybe she should want justice, but she didn't. She just wanted to leave this whole world behind her.

"I need my belt," Scout said, and Tucker blinked in surprise. "I can't leave without it. Can you get it for me?"

"You can have it back," Tucker said. "But why do you have to go? Why can't you stay? You can help us fight for justice."

"It sounds more like revenge to me," Scout said.

"Maybe against the Space Farers it is," Tucker admitted. "They had no call dropping those rocks. But our own government also needs to be held accountable. That gun they're building, just like the others they built before, is technically illegal. It violates the agreement signed between the original colonists on the surface and the support crew up in space. We can hold them accountable. That's justice."

Scout had to admit he had a point. But she didn't have to admit it out loud.

"Can't you stay?" he pleaded again. "Stay with us."

"No," Scout said, blinking back another prickle in her eyes. "No, I can't do that. I would never feel safe working with Malcolm. He's really unstable."

"Malcolm isn't in charge," Tucker said, trying to catch her elbow, but she twisted her arm out of his reach. "Listen—sorry you have to hear it this way, Reggie—he's not going to be in charge here much longer. He *is* unstable. He might be okay again someday, but he can't be in charge anymore, not now. Not with all this about to go down. He's going to be replaced."

Scout wondered if that was even remotely true, but she decided it wasn't really the issue.

"Then there's the matter of you," Scout said. "No force in this galaxy would ever persuade me to trust you again."

"I told you why I did everything I did," Tucker said.

"I don't believe you," Scout said. "I think you do as you like and find reasons to explain it all away later, and I don't want any part of it. I'm leaving."

"You don't know me yet," Tucker insisted.

"I don't intend to, ever," Scout said. "You can be as angry about that as you like, but I don't owe you anything." She turned back to Reggie. "The compound is back that way, past all those stalactites?"

Reggie nodded. "You'll be behind the warehouse."

"Thanks. Hold the dogs until I get back?"

He nodded again. Scout turned to brush past Tucker, but he caught her upper arm and held her tightly, leaning so close to her ear his lips brushed against the outer curve.

"You felt something too. Don't you owe yourself the chance to find out what it was?"

Scout scowled and tried to twist her arm free of his gasp. She could feel her face flushing and saw a look of triumph dawning on Tucker's own face. She *had* felt something. That was the worst part. She would always remember that moment of perfect bliss. His betrayal had marred it but not destroyed it. Even now it called to her.

Tucker's hand reached for her cheek. She supposed he intended to brush her hair back from her face, maybe to touch his fingertips to her cheekbone. To draw her closer.

Whatever he intended, he never got the chance. His hand snapped back and disappeared from view. Then Scout stumbled back as he doubled over, howling in pain. At first, she couldn't tell what was happening.

Then Joelle straightened up from where she was standing behind him, holding his arm locked at what looked like a painful angle up behind his own back. She jerked it up tighter and he fell to his knees.

"Sorry to interrupt," Joelle said to Scout, "but don't you have someplace to be?"

"Yes," Scout said. "Yes, I do."

20

TUCKER TRIED to get back to his feet, but Joelle raised the pinned arm ever higher and he desisted with a squawk of pain. The corner of Joelle's mouth curled up in a self-satisfied grin. He was very much at her mercy. The bare muscles of her arms hardly even tensed as she kept him on his knees.

"Jo," Reggie said, "she needs her belt before she can go."

"I need that belt or I *can't* go," Scout corrected.

Joelle nodded, but her face was grim. "It's with Ken, not my father. Ken will give it to you, but you can't let my father see you. We've been doing everything we can to keep him focused on the data you were carrying, but sooner or later he's going to remember he wanted to do a full interrogation. You have to be gone before then."

"I will be," Scout said. "I'm sorry if I misjudged you."

"You thought I was the 'just following orders' type?" Joelle asked.

"Well, yeah," Scout said. "I mean, he's your dad."

"I'm loyal to my cause," Joelle said. "I'm still loyal to my cause. But my father..." She trailed off, looking at Reggie still hugging the dogs. "My father needs a break," she finished. Not, Scout sensed, the way she had intended to. "Reggie, you need to get back before you're supposed to be waking up. You're running out of time."

"But the dogs," Reggie said.

"Hold on," Joelle said, and Tucker gave another hiss of pain as she shifted her hold on him, then forced him to the ground. She kept a knee on his back as she took a tie from her belt pouch and cinched it around his wrists a bit more snugly than Scout would have done.

"What happens to Tucker?" Scout asked despite herself. Joelle raised an eyebrow as she took hold of the dogs' collars without getting off of Tucker's back. "I mean, if your father is stepping down—"

"Tucker is mine now," Joelle said, the corner of her mouth curling up once more.

Scout wouldn't trade places with Tucker for all the riches in the galaxy.

"Come on," Reggie said, "this way."

"See you in a few," Scout said, and Joelle gave a nod.

"She's really mad," Reggie whispered to Scout as they wound their way through the maze of stalactites.

"If what you say about Tucker sowing discord between her and your father is true, and she knows about it, I can see why," Scout said.

"Discord," Reggie said wonderingly. "Nice word."

Beyond the stalactites was a very narrow tunnel that twisted just at the end before it slipped out into the open space at the bottom of the ramp that led up to the top of the ridge. Scout wasn't surprised she hadn't noticed it before. Even knowing it was there, it was hard to spot.

The first light of dawn was filling the bottom of the ramp with a gray light. She didn't have much time.

"Come on," Reggie said, leading the way back to the warehouse. Scout saw no sign of the door to the cell she had been trapped in. She wasn't even sure what side of the warehouse it would come off of; the natural chambers she had passed through to get back up here had been so irregular in shape and nearly stacked on top of each other her sense of direction had no hope of compensating.

Reggie stopped at the refrigeration units. "The stairs to the dorms are over there," he said, pointing to a dark corner of the warehouse.

"I can take it from here," Scout told him. "Your sister said Ken had my belt."

"Either he's fixing something out in the yard with Bente or he's working on one of the computers in the equipment room."

"Probably the latter if he's working on my stolen data," Scout guessed. "Thanks for all the help. You're a good kid. I hope your dad turns out okay in the end."

"Me too," Reggie said, although he sounded miserable, like he didn't quite believe his father would be okay. "Maybe I should get a dog for him, do you think?"

"Dogs are very good for calming angry or scared thoughts," Scout said from perhaps more experience than she would like to admit. "A dog would definitely be good for you. And there's no such thing as having too many dogs."

Reggie gave her a genuine smile, then dug into his pocket to fetch the plastic whistle and pressed it into her hand. "You might need to use this again."

"Thanks," Scout said. He grinned again, then turned to run up the stairs. She watched until she saw his body outlined by the lantern still in his hands disappear down the hallway at the top of the stairs, then stepped past the refrigeration units to peek into the kitchen. Empty. She tiptoed across to the hallway that ran between the offices.

She could hear voices. She pressed her back against the wall and took a quick darting glance around the corner into the hallway. Two of the office windows were lit up, but the voices were all coming from the one on the left. She could hear the deep rumble of Malcolm's voice, the occasional quieter tones of Arvid, and a third voice that sounded downright robotic.

Scout leaned into the hallway again. The door to the office on the right was open, but she was pretty sure it was empty. The door on the left was closed. If she stayed low and quiet, she should be able to slip past.

Scout crept down the hallway, only dropping to her hands and knees when she approached the lit-up window. The voices were still muffled by the closed door. When Arvid spoke she couldn't make out a word, but Malcolm was growing angry and speaking more loudly, something about the big gun and the stations up in space and time being short.

The other voice, the robotic one, was coming through speakers turned up loud enough to make the door handle rattle as it vibrated with the deep bass.

"This is well in hand, Malcolm," the voice said. "Your further interference is not needed."

"Interference?" There was a bang, like a fist on the metal surface of a desk.

"Do not forget yourself, Malcolm," the voice said. "You have your place and I have mine. I see a bigger picture than you do. You will do as you're told."

Scout was desperately tempted to peek through the glass, but that was far too risky. She had a hunch that whoever was communicating with Malcolm was scrambling their voice and, if they were on videophone, their image as well. Did not even Malcolm know who he was taking orders from?

"This could all be over—" Malcolm said, but the voice interrupted.

"Now is not the time. Do not forget, we have people in space. There is no call to sacrifice them without cause."

Then Arvid spoke again, too softly for Scout to hear, and she crept on, past the window to the equipment room.

Where Ken crouched, watching her approach on all fours.

"Hey," he said. "Joelle tells me you're here for the belt."

"Joelle tells you?"

Ken held up his wrist so she could see the screen strapped there. "Since that little communications mishap with Bente and I not getting Tucker's message on time, we all have communicators now."

"Okay," Scout said, getting to her feet. "The belt?"

"Here it is," Ken said, holding it out for her. "I'm afraid the gun is missing. Malcolm has it in his office. I'm sorry, this is all my fault. I sure hope you don't intend a drastic rescue of your gun."

"No," Scout said, buckling the belt around her waist.

"Because I can give you another gun if you want. Not so shiny, maybe."

"I'm good," Scout said, tapping her palm on the tablet. "I have what I need."

"Oh, good," Ken said with a wide grin. "I was afraid I was going to have to talk you out of being crazy. And hey, sorry for driving you into the canyon wall last night."

"I'm not sure I'm quite at 'forgive and forget' just yet," Scout admitted. "But if you can settle for no hard feelings? Provided, of course, our paths don't cross again."

"Good enough for me," Ken said, putting out a hand.

She hesitated, but gave it a shake. "One last thing," she said, and the smile melted from his face. "The data disks?"

"You still want those?" Ken said.

"I think so, yeah."

Ken turned back to the computer console and searched through a random collection of protein bar wrappers and empty mugs before he found first one and then the other.

"You know we already have all of it on our computer systems," he said. "And it's been beamed to command, probably even into space."

"I figured as much," Scout said. "But still, I'd feel better with these back."

"This information is going to change things," he said.

"Maybe not for the better."

"Well, it can't go on like this forever, can it? Something has to change."

Scout looked at the data disks resting on the palm of her hand, then stuck them back in her pocket. "I really don't know."

"Bente wanted me to tell you best of luck," Ken said. "Truly. Joelle says you're definitely not going to be one of us, which is a shame because we all really liked you. You would have been an asset."

Scout just nodded. She had waited her whole life for the rebels to find her, to make her one of them. She thought that was why her father had sent her on a delivery to the next town on that fateful day when the rock from space had destroyed her whole city. He must have known something. She must have had a destiny.

Gertrude had convinced her how wrong that was. Having a destiny didn't lend meaning to the senseless tragedy of losing her entire family, her home, everything in one blow. She could only give it meaning for herself by her own actions.

She didn't know what that was yet. She thought it probably waited for her out closer to the galactic center, so that was where she was headed.

Now, finally seeing the life she had always thought she wanted, she wasn't sure exactly what she was feeling. It was a sort of melancholy as she looked back at her former self and considered how easily she would have gotten caught up in something that to her current self was clearly a quagmire of politics, with no good guys or bad guys and no clear sign of the right path.

Also an aching sort of awareness of what a narrow escape she had just had. Because only six days separated her former self from her current self. Six days! It felt like a lifetime.

"You better hurry," Ken said. "The big boss likes to keep these calls short. You don't have much time."

"Do you know who—"

Ken cut her off. "Not even a theory. Now go. And good luck!"

Scout hitched her belt up, which it absolutely didn't need since it had adjusted to the size of her waist the minute she had put it on. They had such lovely technology in the galactic center. Then she crawled back down the hallway as quickly as she could. She only heard Arvid and Malcolm arguing with each other behind the closed door and guessed that Ken was right and the call had ended. They could come back out at any time.

She rose to a crouch and ran at the earliest opportunity, not slowing down until she had gone so deeply into the warehouse the light from the kitchen was no longer penetrating to show her the obstacles around her.

Reggie had taken the lantern with him, but Scout had a flashlight on her belt. She quickly found it and switched it on, then continued on through the warehouse to the natural cavern and back through the tangle of stalactites to the larger cave beyond.

There was no one there. No sign of Joelle or her captive Tucker, and no sign of Scout's dogs.

21

SCOUT STOOD COMPLETELY STILL, tilting her head as she listened. She held her breath and tried to slow the heartbeat that was pounding too loudly in her ears. Somewhere, not remotely close by, she could hear a drip of water. Even more distantly, she thought she heard the hum of machinery.

Then she heard a snuffle.

"Shadow! Gert!" she called. Then she remembered the whistle in her pocket and took it out to give it a blow.

The dogs came charging out from behind a rock outcropping. Shadow was trembling as he leapt into her arms and even Gert looked torn between deep upset and elation at seeing her again.

What had happened since she left? And where were Joelle and Tucker?

Scout sat down on the cave floor so the dogs could cuddle close to her while she put the eyepiece over her left eye and consulted the tablet. There were no new messages. She brought up the coordinates Liam had sent her on the map display and studied the terrain between that dot and her current location.

If the mining tunnel let out where Reggie said it would, she would find herself on top of the ridge on the far side of the canyon behind the compound. From there, it was a long, shallow slope to the prairie floor. An easy walk from there to the meeting point, nothing to jump over or navigate around. She would be there in time.

If she left right now.

Scout scratched at the dogs as she looked at the cave floor around her. The bare rock gave no clue what had happened to Joelle and Tucker.

She didn't think Joelle would leave the dogs unattended without reason. She had already had Tucker subdued and was settled in to wait. So either Tucker had gotten the upper hand or someone had summoned her away.

And yet she had seen no sign of either of them between here and the compound. So where could they have gone?

Scout sighed and pushed the dogs away to get back on her feet. She hated not knowing, and she worried that Joelle might need help, but the fact was if she didn't get moving, she was going to miss meeting Liam. She couldn't risk that, especially not after everything she had done to get this far.

"Come, dogs," Scout said and crossed the cave to the red glow outlining the mining tunnel.

She hoped she wasn't going to regret this moment forever.

Reggie had been right about the tunnel. It ran straight and true, the sandy floor smooth and even. The tunnel pierced through natural caverns from time to time, but there was never any danger of losing the path.

Scout kept the dogs close to her side, not running ahead or falling behind, and her eyes scanned every rock formation that could hide an ambush, but the walk was uneventful. Joelle and Tucker might have gone back into the compound, or up to the top of the ridge, or deeper into the caverns that led to the escape vent from the cell, but Scout was beginning to doubt they had gone down this tunnel before her.

There was a patch of bright light ahead and Scout switched off the flashlight and stowed it on her belt. The light gained definition, becoming a golden beam of sunshine illuminating a rickety old ladder that led up to the surface.

Dogs weren't much good with ladders.

"Gert, stay," Scout said, picking up Shadow and tucking him under her arm. It was a bit awkward climbing the ladder with only one hand and her feet, but she only had to go three or four meters before she was out in the sunshine.

Scout tipped her head, squinting against the blinding sun, then looked around. She wasn't quite at the top of the ridge. But she was at the bottom of a narrow channel between two broken rock faces that led up to the top of the ridge. It would be a steep climb, but it wasn't far.

Scout set Shadow down on the ground. "Stay, Shadow," she said. He sat down, then lowered himself until he was sitting sphinxlike to wait for her return.

Scout climbed back down the ladder and then stood looking at Gert. Gert, who was twice the size of Shadow. Gert, whom she couldn't exactly carry tucked under one arm even if she cooperated, which Scout doubted she would do. How was she going to get her up to the surface?

Scout turned her attention back to the ladder. It was barely attached to the wall by two sets of screws. She grabbed the bottom rung and gave it a pull until the lower screws pulled free from the crumbling rock. She had to back up and pull harder to get the top screws to give way, and by the time she had done it, her arms were trembling from the exertion.

But she could now move the ladder. She set it against the wall so that instead of going straight up to the edge of the opening, it met the wall at an angle about a meter below. She leaned on it with all her weight, afraid it might slip at the bottom. It did slip a few centimeters, and then it caught fast against a ridge in the floor.

She tested it with her weight again, then stepped up onto it. It was holding, not even wobbling, but anxiety still ate at her stomach. If it gave way when she was near the top, it was going to hurt.

"Here, Gert," Scout said, crouching to take the big dog in her arms. Gert was a beast, but being on the ladder was making her nervous as well. She clung close to Scout's chest, pressing her head against the side of Scout's neck. Scout tightened her arms around the dog, then put one foot and then the other forward. It was still a steep climb, and she had to focus to keep her balance, but it was doable.

She reached the top of the ladder and looked up into the sunlight. Gert resisted her first attempt to push the dog up the side of the wall and Scout's stomach did a somersault as Gert's frantic twisting nearly sent them both tumbling off the ladder.

Then Shadow barked, the outline of his head appearing over the side of the hole, and Gert whimpered, wanting to be with her friend.

Scout gritted her teeth and tried lifting Gert up into the air again. Her arms were still trembling from pulling the ladder free, but Gert was cooperating, staying as still as she could until Scout had her high enough for her front paws to touch the ground above. Then she clawed frantically and Scout got both her hands under Gert's hindquarters and somehow the dog was up and away, barking and dancing with Shadow in the sunshine.

Scout pressed her head to the wall of the shaft and waited for her arm muscles to recover.

If she had to, she could climb back down and set the ladder more vertically so it ended closer to the surface, but Scout was suddenly very anxious not to go back down into that dark hole. She was done with lurking underground; she hoped forever.

At last she reached up, finding a firm hold for each hand. Then she groped first with one foot and then the other to find holds a little higher up for her toes. The holds were shallow, but scraping at the walls with her boots didn't help her find any more higher up. She was running out of options.

The trembling was back in her arms. Either she was going to have to quit or she was going to have to hurry. Scout gave a mighty yell, then forced her muscles to do her bidding, pulling herself up and over the edge.

She rolled out of the hole and lay flat on her back to catch her breath. It wasn't hot, not yet, but she could sense already that she was going to be regretting her lack of water by the time she reached Liam.

The real work of the day hadn't even started yet. It was too soon to be this exhausted.

Scout hiked herself up on her elbows and then to a sitting position. Her arms ached terribly and barely functioned at all when she lifted them up to push back her sweaty hair. Luckily, she wasn't going to be needing them to walk.

She got to her feet and whistled for the dogs, who came running to her, tongues lolling out of their mouths.

"This way, dogs," she said, leading the way up the steep, narrow channel between the two rock faces. It was like those two towering cliffs had butted heads a long time ago, grinding away at each other, filling the space between with bits of themselves. The footing was none too steady and Scout found it slow going, not the least because once again she needed to use her arms to keep her balance.

The dogs had an easier time, racing past her to the top of the ridge. She could hear them playing up there, occasionally taking breaks to go back to the top of the channel and look down at her and her slow progress before returning to their game.

By the time she reached the top she was bathed in sweat, moisture she could little afford to lose. She told herself again that the rest of the walk would be easier. She whistled for the dogs to rejoin her and they came charging out of a stand of scrubby grass to her side.

Shadow sat next to her, looking up at her for further orders. Gert, as usual, was distracted by something else. Scout saw the bristles forming up Gert's back and her low growl was building to a deep woof when she suddenly gave a hurt-filled whine and fell to the ground.

"Gert?" Scout dropped to a knee, running her hands over the dog's dark fur. What had just happened?

Then Shadow staggered back from the edge and fell drunkenly to his side.

Standing out starkly against his white fur was a tiny needlelike dart.

Scout looked back down the channel to see Tucker standing halfway up the steep slope with a rifle aimed at her.

"Don't move, Scout," he said. "Why don't you stand up and keep your hands where I can see them?"

"Why should I?" she shouted, her voice magnified as it bounced back down the channel.

"Your dogs will be fine. I even calibrated the dosages for their sizes. I'm not here to hurt any of you."

"Where's Joelle?" she demanded.

"Joelle is fine. She's back at the compound with her father. I can message her if you like. Why don't you come back down here and we can do that?"

"I'm not going back down," Scout said, still crouched over Gert. She found the dart in the dog's dark fur and plucked it out, then did the same for Shadow. She wasn't sure if that would even help.

"You're not leaving," Tucker said. "Believe me, it would be better if you came with me."

"What's the alternative?"

"Malcolm has us chase you down on the motorcycles. Those guns don't fire darts."

"How just like you, always coming at me with the kinder option," Scout said.

"I'm glad you recognize that."

"I was being sarcastic."

"I thought as much, but I figured I'd give you a chance to be sincere."

Scout laughed, a harsh sound as it echoed around them. "I'm not the one with a sincerity problem."

"I can explain everything," he said. He kept the rifle trained on her, but started to continue the long climb up to the top of the ridge.

"I don't need an explanation," Scout said. "I just need to go. You have everything. Why can't you just let me go?"

"Do we, Scout?" he asked. He was making much quicker work of the climb than she had and was getting too close, too fast. "Do we really have everything? More to the point, do we really know everything that you know? Or is there something more, something that still might help us with our mission?"

"I didn't even know what was on those disks," Scout said.

"Stand up," he said, stopping a few meters short of the edge. "Leave your dogs, they're fine. Just take a few more steps back, but keep your hands where I can see them."

Scout narrowed her eyes at him, but she was all too aware of the rifle barrel bearing down on her. She got up and stepped backwards slowly. She kept her hands up, palms out, but close to her hips.

Just as Gertrude had always done. Only she had always had her pistol on her. Scout had lost that just when she suspected she would no longer have qualms about using it.

"I honestly don't understand why you want to leave," Tucker said. "We're a family here, and you could be a part of that. Don't you want to be a part of that?"

"Not that family," Scout said.

"I know Malcolm is taking things a little hard, getting a little heated up. We all know that. I was supposed to fetch something he needs from McFarlane, but as you know, there wasn't anything there. And without it, he gets a little... his emotions run a little hotter than normal. But he's going to be getting help now. The big boss has spoken to Arvid and Joelle about it. Someone is coming to take his place here, and then Malcolm is going to rest for a while back in the city."

"You think my problem with this situation is confined to Malcolm giving fiery speeches?" Scout asked.

"What else could it be?" he asked, sounding genuinely confused. "Politics?"

"It's you, you idiot. You lied to me. You betrayed me. There's no way you're ever coming back from that in my eyes. I don't forgive stuff like that."

"I told you, I can explain," he said.

"And I told you I didn't want to hear your explanations," Scout said. "I know how good you are with talking. You say all sorts of things that sound true, and maybe you even believe them when you're saying them. I don't know. But they won't be true forever. They will only be true until you need something else to be true."

"That's crazy talk."

"Is it, Tucker? You swore to me you never set foot in McFarlane's hut until I went inside, but tell me true. I just saw you shoot both my tiny little dogs from quite a long range with that dart gun. You didn't need to go inside that hut to kill him, did you? Then you saw me coming and stashed the gun before revealing yourself. Am I close?"

Tucker didn't answer for a long time. Finally, he responded with a barely audible, "You don't know me."

"I know enough to know that I don't want to," Scout said. "Ever."

Tucker stared at her for a long moment and Scout braced herself for an explosion of maniacal laughter or angry words or even excessive weeping.

In the end he threw his head back and bellowed rage at the sky. But it didn't really matter what he did to vent his emotions. Because at the same time, the barrel of the rifle swayed away from her, and that was all the opening she needed.

Gertrude's gun might be tucked away somewhere in Malcolm's office, but Scout had made it through a rough lifetime without such things.

A slingshot and a pocketful of stones had always been enough for her, and they didn't let her down this time. Tucker's howl of rage ended abruptly, and he fell back against the rock face behind him. His eyes were already losing focus as he slowly slumped to the ground. His gaze found hers as if through a fog only he could see. His gray eyes were full of hurt at what he considered her sudden betrayal. His lips worked as if he was trying to speak her name, but couldn't get a breath to form a sound.

Scout was unmoved. She waited for the rifle to fall from his grasp before rushing to him, seizing the gun and throwing it with all her might into the depths of the canyon.

Then she looked down at Tucker. She had hit him square in the forehead, a nice match for the lump she still sported over her right eye.

He was turning gray. Scout dropped to her knees and grabbed his wrist to feel for a pulse.

He wasn't dead. Still, she could have killed him. Very easily.

Too easily. Apparently, it didn't even matter whether she had a gun in her hand or not. She was capable of murder with nothing more than a rock.

Who was she becoming?

Scout pushed the thoughts aside. She would have time later for self-examination. Right now, Tucker likely needed some basic first aid. Not that she wanted to linger to provide it to him, not after he had shot both her dogs, but she could at least call for help. She turned his wrist over in her hands. He was still wearing his comm screen like the others. Scout touched it to bring it to life, then scrolled through the list of names until she got to Joelle's. She opened a text window and tapped away at the screen.

JOELLE TUCKER IS HURT IM LEAVING HIM JUST UPHILL FROM THE MINING TUNNEL EXIT CAN YOU COME GET HIM

While she waited for a response, she helped herself to the contents of Tucker's pockets. That much felt like justice. He had nothing she needed. Her own utility knife was more elaborate than his and had been tucked into one of the belt pouches after they had taken it from her. His tablet was much like the one she had taken from McFarlane, nothing to compare to Gertrude's, which, among other features, contained its own compass. He did have a flask at the back of his belt, half empty. She took a tentative sip but found it to be just water. Not much, but she could make it last.

She had just secured the flask in a pouch on her own belt when she saw Joelle's response appearing letter by letter on the comm screen.

ILL GET HIM YOU BETTER GET MOVING KEN AND BENTE CAN ONLY PRETEND NOT TO FIND YOU FOR SO LONG BEST OF LUCK

Scout responded with the single letter K, then climbed back up to the top of the ridge.

She could hear engines in the distance. She looked to the south, across the narrow canyon to the ridge she had stood on with Tucker less than a day before, then beyond that to the canyon where she had left her rover smashed into the canyon wall. She could just make out two plumes of dust. Ken and Bente, looking in what they knew was the wrong place.

Scout looked down at her dogs. How long would the darts' effects last?

She didn't have time to waste finding out. She had to get moving. Sooner or later Ken and Bente would have to check this canyon, and when they did, she wanted to be already deep into the cover of the prairie grasses.

Scout took off her long sun-protective shirt and spread it out on the ground, then laid Gert's limp body in the center of it. The shirt looked thin, even felt thin in the way it let air pass through it, but it was far sturdier than it looked. It would get Scout through one more morning, if not serving quite its intended purpose.

Scout laid back without crushing Gert, then found the sleeves and tied them tightly across her chest. It took a bit of adjusting to make a sling Gert wouldn't slip out of, and it was a struggle to get to her knees and then stagger to her feet with the heavy dog across her back, but once she was up, it wasn't too bad.

She had to crouch down again, this time to gather Shadow up into her arms. Her thighs ached at the strain of rising up with the weight of one dog across her back and another clutched close to her chest, but she managed.

Then she turned toward the rising sun and started taking one step after another, keeping her head down. She regretted the loss of her hat, not just for sentimental reasons; she had no way now to block out the light.

One step after another. That was all she needed to do. Keep putting one foot in front of the other until her journey was done.

22

SCOUT GREW MORE and more stooped as the hours dragged on. She kept putting one foot in front of the other, the entirety of her plan, but neither dog was showing any sign of waking. Shadow's fur clung itchily to her sweaty skin and Gert was a dead weight on her back.

The mere fact of Gert's weight wasn't the worst part of having to carry her. The worst part was that she had used her shirt for the sling, which left her arms and chest unprotected from the harsh rays from the sun. Her lower legs were exposed as well. All of her clothes were shorts because long pants didn't work out well for her on her bike, but until today she had always been meticulous with her use of sunscreen.

But that sunscreen was in her saddlebags, with her bike and her father's hat, back in the crashed rover.

She had begun to feel the first tingles of impending burn mere minutes after she had started walking. It was better here in the tall prairie grasses, but now that the sun was climbing up near its apex, she once more had no shade. Only this time the rays were pounding down on already bright red skin.

Her only hope was that when she reached Liam, he had some sort of medical equipment that could help her. She would never be able to sleep; she was burned deeply from every angle.

At least the sounds of motorcycle engines were gone now. They had drawn closer not long after she had waded into the grassy sea, but they were focusing their search on the canyons, not the prairie. And now that she was in the depths of the tall grass, they would have to be on top of her to find her. Even burdened with two unconscious dogs as she was, barely plodding along, she left very little wake behind her. The grass fell back into place without bending or losing a grain and her boots left no mark on the hard packed ground.

Scout's mouth had gone from sticky to completely dry, and she was not replacing the sweat that had evaporated off her skin. She wanted very badly to take a sip from Tucker's flask, but she was afraid if she set Shadow down, she would never get him up into her arms again. She would just melt down to the ground and give up.

She would never let herself do that.

She put the flask out of her mind and focused on the toes of her boots, all she could see past the dog in her arms. Left foot, right foot, left foot, right foot, over and over.

Her brain bounced between those two thoughts on an endless loop for some time. The plethora of insects that lived in the sea of grass around her began to fall silent, as they always did in the middle of the day. It was too hot now, even for them. In her bike delivery days, she would have stopped before now, either found shelter or created her own shade with the blanket she carried in her saddlebag. Then she and the dogs would sip water, nap, and wait for the heat to begin to abate.

The world around her was getting hazy. Some of that was the sun, but some of it was starting to scare her. She absolutely couldn't afford to faint now. She focused back on her feet.

A low rumble rolled across the prairie. Scout's first thought was that it was another earthquake, but the ground beneath her was quite still. Then she thought thunder, but there was not a cloud in the sky.

By while she was looking up at the sky, she saw a white arc tracing across the deep blue, growing thicker as it curved down. She thought at first it was going to arc down to the horizon, but it didn't. It was growing thicker and something was flashing brightly. Reflecting the sun or creating its own white heat? She couldn't tell.

A stab of fear made her stumble, and she fell to her knees, spilling

Shadow to the ground. She gripped her own thighs, forcing herself to take deep breaths.

She had been near enough to her city when it was destroyed to be blown off her bike by the shock wave, but she had been pedaling away from it. She had never seen the rock as it fell from the sky as Tucker had. But how could it have looked like anything but what she was staring at now?

The object in the sky flashed again. Were the Space Farers now just dropping the magnetic shield satellites down to the surface rather than simply dismantling them? Two attacks in one?

But the object in the sky suddenly changed its trajectory, the arc becoming a straight line as it slowed down. The rumble became a roar and the fear in Scout's heart became grateful joy.

It was Liam. It had to be. He was landing his spacecraft at the rendezvous point.

Scout took out her tablet to see how far away she still was, glancing up again and again as the flashing light drew closer and started forming distinct parts. Definitely a ship of some sort, metallic, with several small engines firing to slow its descent.

She was nearly there. She opened the messaging part of the tablet and told him so, and asked him to please wait.

She was just tucking the eyepiece back in her pocket when Shadow made a little whimper. Scout gently lifted his head to see him groggily opening his eyes. She took out the flask and poured just a bit into her cupped hand and held it out for him to lick it clean. He was becoming more alert by the minute.

Gert on her back was stirring as well, and Scout sat back until the dog was on the ground and then untied the sleeves. Gert struggled out of the sling, crawling over to get her own sip of water. By the time they were both done, there were only a few drops left for Scout, but she didn't mind.

The roar was loud now, and the dogs couldn't see where it was coming from. From their perspective, the whole world was grass. They cowered close to Scout even as she got to her feet up on tiptoes to see over the grass.

She had seen pictures and videos of spacecraft in her history classes when she had still been in school. The craft before her was nothing like those. Its metallic hull gleamed dully in the sunlight all along its needlelike fuselage.

Like the rover, the spacecraft her ancestors had favored had been utilitarian and built to last. This delicate thing looked like a strong wind would blow it away. And as she watched, three little feet extended out, one at the nose and two at the mildly wider rear. It settled down to disappear in the grass.

Then there was silence.

"Come on, dogs," Scout said, picking up her shirt and leading the way through the grass. She set a pace they could keep up with—not as fast as she'd like to be moving, but there was no way she was going to try carrying them again.

She was expecting to find the large, flattened circle in the grain that happened when a ship from space made an emergency landing, but clearly this craft differed from what she was familiar with in more than just cosmetics. Its engines had been firing. She had seen the glow as it descended, and yet nothing on the ground was singed or even bent over from the blast. One minute she was surrounded by grass, and the next she was still surrounded by grass but with one hand pressed against the burning hot metal of the craft's hull.

She yelped and snatched her hand back.

"Hello?" a voice called.

Both of the dogs started barking at the potential danger the voice might be bringing with it. She shushed them, then shouted, "It's me, Scout Shannon."

"Scout Shannon!" the voice called back. Then a man suddenly appeared beside her in the grass. He had the palest skin Scout had ever seen and thin wisps of ginger-blond hair that left far too much of his scalp exposed.

"You need to get out of the sun," Scout said.

"It looks like you needed to get out of the sun some time ago," he countered. "Are you all right?"

"I will be," she said. "Can we go inside? I could really use some water."

"Of course. The ramp is over here."

He guided her around the nose of the craft to a small ramp, really a staircase, so steep that once more Scout was compelled to lift her dogs to get them up it.

The inside of the craft was chilly; that was her first impression. It was also very small, smaller even than the rover. Liam climbed up behind her, brushing past her to touch the back wall of the craft's interior. Something slid out of the wall. Scout only realized it was a sink when he made water start pouring out of it. The dogs, still thirsty, ran to investigate. He slid open a panel and found a bowl to fill for them, then a glass to fill and bring to Scout.

"It's just you?" Scout asked, looking around the ship as she sipped her water. There was only one seat at the controls in the front and nothing else to be seen in the back but the chrome walls crisscrossed with lines like a grid. She guessed anything you needed would slide out of certain parts of the walls like the sink and the cabinet had. Very space-efficient.

"Yes, I had to come alone," he told her. "This planet is off-limits."

"To marshals?"

"To anyone. That's why I had to be so terse in my messages to you. I was doing all I could to disguise where you were sending from and where I was replying to. It seems like it worked, but..." He broke off with a shrug. Scout could see his pale skin beginning to pinken with an impending burn.

"If you got caught, you'd be fired?"

"Fired and likely thrown in prison."

"Why?"

"It's disputed territory. It's forbidden for galactic citizens to take sides, and coming here makes it look like I'm choosing sides."

"Because you came down to the surface?"

He looked at her with deep puzzlement for some time before shaking his head. "I see. Gertrude mentioned a little altercation going on here. No, that's not the problem. The surface-versus-orbit dispute isn't what I'm referring to."

"What are you referring to?"

"It doesn't matter," Liam said briskly. "You're here now. I can disappear with no one the wiser, so it really doesn't matter."

"Oh," Scout said, realizing he must be in a hurry to go. She set the glass on the edge of the sink, then took off Gertrude's belt to hand it to him. "I'm sorry, someone stole the gun from me, but I can return the rest of her things."

Liam looked confused again, but took the belt and set it behind the pilot's seat. "Thanks. Having that back might take a little of the heat off with my boss."

"Before you go, I have something else," Scout said, digging in her pocket for the two disks. "These were stolen, too. I got them back, but the data fell into the wrong hands first. I think..." She had to stop as her throat tried to close on her. She hadn't realized she was this upset about it, but when she heard her own next words, she knew they were true, even though she had not been allowing herself to even think them until now. "I think I may have just started a war."

"I see," Liam said, taking the disks from her. He summoned a computer terminal out of one of the walls and plugged both data disks into it. The decryption was instantaneous, and in a flash, they were both looking at gun specs, status reports of satellites being taken down, and census data. "War has been brewing for a while now here, hasn't it?" he asked as he scrolled through the data.

"Yes," Scout said, her voice still thick.

"And this all just fell into your lap?"

"Two of the women Gertrude and I were trapped with were dabbling in espionage," Scout said. "On opposite sides, I think. There seem to be at least three sides. I don't know. It's all very complicated."

"Clearly," Liam said, his eyes still on the data-filled screen. Then he switched it off with a click and turned to her. "I'm not very familiar with the situation here, but it's evidently far worse than the picture I've been drawing from what little info I had. But don't fret. We will figure something out. But we definitely can't fix this from here."

"Okay," Scout said miserably.

"I have connections back at the galactic center who can help. Who will want to help," he added, trying to catch her downcast eyes. "Sometimes war is inevitable, but sometimes it isn't. My friends are working hard to avert this one. And they can do amazing things. They got me here, beyond the blockade where I was never supposed to be. They can help with this."

"Okay," Scout said, a bit more surely.

"Now, they are anxious to meet you, and I'm anxious to get out of this no-man's-land. So, Scout Shannon, are you ready to leave all this behind and come to the galactic center with me?"

The fear for the fate of the people on her planet didn't leave her, but she managed to tuck it further back in her mind and give him a genuine smile.

"I am. I'm so ready to go."

He touched another wall and summoned a second chair for her to strap into. It was built for someone much larger than she was, larger even than Liam was, so there was room for Shadow and Gert to both hop up beside her. She wrapped an arm around each and gave them each a kiss for good luck.

Finally, *finally*, she was going into space. An entire galaxy waited for her. And she was so ready for it.

She was ready for anything.

CHECK OUT BOOK THREE!

The Travels of Scout Shannon continues in Book Three, Among Treacherous Stars.

Scout Shannon wants nothing more than to leave her home world and its petty squabbling factions behind. Galactic central with all of its excitement and opportunities awaits her.

She makes it as far as her own planet's orbit before the snares of bureaucracy close around her, trapping her on a space station populated by her people's oldest foe. Then her rescuer, her only friend in the galaxy, disappears, abducted by a group of strangers the moment he steps off his ship.

Alone in a strange place, surrounded by the old enemies she knows and new enemies just making themselves known, Scout faces a challenge like none before. But with her dogs at her side, Scout stands prepared for anything.

"Among Treacherous Stars" the third book in "The Travels of Scout Shannon" series, a young adult science fiction novel for fans of plucky heroines, girl spies conspiring in political intrigues, and loyal dog sidekicks.

Among Treacherous Stars, book three in the Travels of Scout Shannon series. Check it out!

NEW SERIES: THE FORGOTTEN PLANET

Coming soon from Ratatoskr Press Books, the new YA sci-fi series THE FORGOTTEN PLANET starts with book 1: Raiding the Forgotten Derelict.

History sleeps beneath them all, but only she sees it.

Lafayette Eloi always knew her parents thought differently from others. They kept their books buried beneath her mother's house. They spoke an old language in the dead of night, whispering behind closed doors and bolted shutters. She grew up in a village where no one was related to her, and she never knew why.

Then, after her mother died, her father came to fetch her. Now she and her mother's dog assist her father in his work. The work discussed in whispers in the dark. The work that had cost Lafayette so much all her young life.

But now she learns just how much her father's work means to their entire world. Only no one knows anything about it. Only her father. And only Lafayette.

Because the work that consumed her father's entire life and her mother's too now nibbles at the fringe's of Lafayette's own life. And she cannot refuse its call.

Raiding the Forgotten Derelict, first book in the new YA sci-fu series THE FORGOTTEN PLANET, available in September 2024 from Ratatoskr Press Books.

COMPLETE SERIES: THE RITCHIE AND FITZ SCI-FI MURDER MYSTERIES

The Ritchie and Fitz Sci-Fi Murder Mysteries starts with Murder on the Intergalactic Railway.

For Murdina Ritchie, acceptance at the Oymyakon Foreign Service Academy means one last chance at her dream of becoming a diplomat for the Union of Free Worlds. For Shackleton Fitz IV, it represents his last chance not to fail out of military service entirely.

Strange that fate should throw them together now, among the last group of students admitted after the start of the semester. They had once shared the strongest of friendships. But that all ended a long time ago.

But when an insufferable but politically important woman turns up murdered, the two agree to put their differences aside and work together to solve the case.

Because the murderer might strike again. But more importantly, solving a murder would just have to impress the dour colonel who clearly thinks neither of them belong at his academy.

Murder on the Intergalactic Railway, the first book in the Ritchie and Fitz Sci-Fi Murder Mysteries.

COMPLETE SERIES: THE TRAVELS OF SCOUT SHANNON

The complete six-book series THE TRAVELS OF SCOUT SHANNON begin with book one, Under Falling Skies.

Scout Shannon's whole family died the day the Space Farers dropped an asteroid on their domed city. Now she lives alone, out in the wild with only her dogs for company. She prefers it that way.

But Scout finds herself at a crossroads. One road leads back to a quiet life snug under the protective dome of a city. The other road leads to a life in the rebellion, a life of adventure and excitement but also danger. Dare she try to find the rebels hiding in the hills?

Then a chance encounter with a stranger from the other side of the galaxy threatens to derail what remains of Scout's life. The entire galaxy awaits her, if she survives the next four days.

"Under Falling Skies", a young adult science fiction novel, set on a remote planet with a distinctly Old West feel. For fans of gunslinging women and young girl assassins. And dogs.

Under Falling Skies, the first book in THE TRAVELS OF SCOUT SHANNON, available everywhere now.

SCI-FI SERIAL PODCAST!

Check out my new monthly podcast of serialized science fiction: THE TALES OF THE CHAI MAKHANI TRIO!

Elyot loathes the massive Commonwealth ships that hover menacingly over his home world of Adghal. He hates the Commonwealth enforcers who harass the populace even more. But with his mother missing and presumed dead, Elyot keeps his head down and strives to avoid notice. And he succeeds until the day two strangers enter his life...

New episodes of this sci-fi serial drop every 1st of the month.

Now streaming on Apple Podcasts, Google Podcasts, Spotify, Stitcher and more. Also available in eBook and print everywhere books or sold. For a complete episode listing, check out the page on my website.

ALSO FROM KATE MACLEOD

Love heists and capers? Then check out my new series, THE VIC HARPER CAPERS. The action starts with the novella THE THIRD POLE JOB.

Vic Harper and her gang retired wealthy from their life of thievery and heists. Whether in a luxury condo overlooking the river in Minneapolis or in a modernist mansion built into the side of a mountain in Colorado, life comes easy now.

Perhaps too easy.

When an old friend asks for a favor his niece, Vic and her mentor Chase Woodward leap at the chance to relieve a little of the boredom. But a quick bit of B&E in a wealthy suburb of Chicago leads to an even greater challenge.

The prize? Nothing much. Just the opportunity to level a playing field for their friend's niece.

But the heist? May prove to be their toughest ever. Because to get to the prize, they'll have to climb a mountain.

And not just any mountain. Their prize waits on the summit of Mount Everest.

THE THIRD POLE JOB, the first novella in the Vic Harper Caper series. For those who love capers, heists and other impossible missions.

ALSO FROM RATATOSKR PRESS

Also from Ratatoskr Press, The Witches Three Cozy Mystery Series by Cate Martin, a mix of mystery and magic that begins with Book 1: Charm School.

Amanda Clarke thinks of herself as perfectly ordinary in every way. Just a small-town girl who serves breakfast all day in a little diner nestled next to the highway, nothing but dairy farms for miles around. She fits in there.

But then an old woman she never met dies, and Amanda was named in her will. Now Amanda packs a bag and heads to the big city, to Miss Zenobia Weekes' Charm School for Exceptional Young Ladies. And it's not in just any neighborhood. No, she finds herself on Summit Avenue in St. Paul, a street lined with gorgeous old houses, the former homes of lumber barons, railroad millionaires, even the writer F. Scott Fitzgerald. Why, Amanda can practically hear the jazz music still playing across the decades.

Scratch that. The music really, literally, still plays in the backyard of the charm school. Because the house stretches across time itself. Without a witch to protect this tear in the fabric of the world, anything can spill over. Like music.

Or like murder.

The complete series is out now, and it all starts with Charm School.

FREE EBOOK!

Like exclusive, free content?

To get two prequel short stories to THE RITCHIE AND FITZ SCI-FI MURDER MYSTERIES as well as a bonus prequel novelette to the completed six-book series THE TRAVELS OF SCOUT SHANNON, signup for my monthly newsletter at KateMacLeodWrites.com.

Thank you!

ABOUT THE AUTHOR

Photograph © 2016 Jonathan Conklin

Kate MacLeod has written stories which have appeared in Analog, Strange Horizons and Mythic Delirium, among other places. She is also the author of two young adult science fictions series: The Travels of Scout Shannon, and The Ritchie and Fitz Sci-Fi Murder Mysteries. She also contributes to a serialized science fiction podcast called The Tales of the Chai Makhani Trio. She currently lives in Minneapolis, Minnesota.

Find out more about the author and sign up for her newsletter at KateMacLeodWrites.com.

ALSO BY KATE MACLEOD

Novels

The Slums of the Solar System:

Mitwa

The Mars of Malcontents

The Whole World for Each

Books 1-3 Box Set

The Travels of Scout Shannon:

Under Falling Skies

In Quaking Hills

Among Treacherous Stars

Against Impassable Barriers

Over Freezing Altitudes

At Galactic Central

The Travels of Scout Shannon Books 1-3

The Travels of Scout Shannon Books 4-6

The Travels of Scout Shannon Books 1-6

The Ritchie and Fitz Sci-Fi Murder Mysteries:

Murder on the Intergalactic Railway

Murder in the Skies

Body in the Catacombs

Death on the Summit

An Undiplomatic Murder

A Lethal Betrayal

The Forgotten Planet

Raiding the Forgotten Derelict (Forthcoming September 2024)

Sci-Fi Novellas

The Intergenerational Tree

I Rise into a Daybreak

Caper Novellas

The Third Pole Job

The Twelve Days of Christmas Job

10-Story Collections

Tales of Blood and Ink

Tales of Old Gods and New

5-Story Collections

Tales from Heian-Kyo and Others

Tales from the Edges and Ends

Tales from Forgotten Days

Tales from Ancient and Future Times

<u>Tales from Across Space</u>